ONLY
TWO

the loss of the *Loch Ard*

a novel

Jackie Randall

A catalogue record for this
book is available from the
NATIONAL
LIBRARY National Library of Australia
OF AUSTRALIA

ISBN: 978-0-9953797-4-9

jr

Thank you Phillip

Some stories are lost to the ravages of
time ... this one will not be.

PROLOGUE

The iron ship howled. It broke somewhere and some of it grazed slowly down the rocks and sent sparks along the cliff that, for seconds, illuminated her fall. Huge rivets launched like dozens of gunshots. The sea surged. The hull scraped along many yards of its length. The screech of metal was deafening. The top masts cracked against the cliff, snapped like twigs, and folded in a slow, wailing motion towards the deck. The last lantern expired. For a moment, there was silence. Then terrible cries for help came from places Tom could not see.

CHAPTER ONE

A rooster crowed from the coop near the foremast and a few passengers and well-wishers glanced his way.

Tom inhaled the steam from the coffee in his mug. He drank in quick gulps then tipped the last grainy drops over the side and watched them merge with the brown of the river. He edged through the crowd to his bunkroom on the main deck and hooked the mug above his bed. When he stepped out, a youth pounced into his path.

'Can I help raise the sails, sir?' the youth asked. He was around fourteen – four or five years younger than Tom. A wiry tangle of dark hair tumbled about his head. His wide eyes danced across Tom's face then paused briefly at the fresh bruising around his eye.

Most voyages began with a few young men itching to play at being sailors but it rarely worked out.

Tom smiled. 'Hello,' he said. 'What's your name?'

'Thomas Carmichael,' the lad said. 'We're emigrating to Australia.' He said "emigrating" as though he was picturing a new adventure of *Gulliver's Travels.* A hasty point with his head hinted portside to a cheerless man and an uneasy woman standing with two young women and two little girls.

Tom shook Thomas's hand. 'I'm Tom Pearce. Too much happening today Thomas, but find me tomorrow and I'll give you some work with the sails.'

'Yes, sir!' Thomas said.

'Don't call me sir,' Tom said. 'I'm just an apprentice. Call me Tom.'

'Yes, Tom!' The boy spun away and almost fell into a cluster of elderly guests. He ducked to the starboard rail and stopped there to gaze out at the busy Thames.

The ship's bell rang for Tom's watch and the second-mate ordered him and other crewmen up the foremast to check every rope and fixture before departure.

An hour later, at noon, the bell rang again. First-Mate McLauchlan – "Mac" – waited at the poop deck rail. Crew stopped their tasks and nudged through the crush of people to stand in four cramped lines below him. From the back line, Tom took a moment to look around.

Passengers and guests stood hushed, watching and curious. Some restless; some eager-eyed. Mac rumbled out quick orders then called the crew roll in random.

'Vedel?'

'Aye!'

'Pearce?'

'Aye!'

'Wright?'

He ticked against each of the three-dozen crew, closed the book, and cast his eyes around the crowd on the deck.

'Please pay attention,' Mac's voice drummed. 'It's my pleasure to introduce Captain George Gibb, the new master of the *Loch Ard*.'

It was Tom's first decent look at Gibb. A stocky man, maybe thirty, with a thick black beard and alert, focused eyes.

'Welcome aboard the *Loch Ard*,' Gibb said. His Scottish burr projected over the breeze and over the buzz of activity on the pier.

Gibb delivered the usual captain's speech. His friendly welcome included the daily schedule at sea: passengers' breakfast would be served at eight, lunch at one, supper at six. The church service would be held on deck every Sunday morning at ten, weather permitting. He listed where passengers were not permitted, then reminded them that all guests must say goodbye and have left the ship by quarter past two.

'But now, all first-class passengers and their guests are to join me for a swift welcome party in the cuddy,' he said and he moved towards the steps.

Mac dismissed everyone. Tom queued with others as they collected their lunch, then he found a seat on a coil of rope. Others sat on barrels or crates. They spooned chunky, steaming potato soup from their mugs and tore bread to soak up the dregs. Some talked. Tom listened to a few discussing Gibb – some doubtful, some hopeful. Tom would wait and see, and he'd lay low until his bruises faded.

This routine of passengers and guests and welcoming and goodbyes was repeated at every departure, only altered by the timing of the tide.

Eventually the guests began to leave. Sisters and mothers shuffled down the gangway to the pier. Some sobbed into embroidered handkerchiefs. Brothers and fathers straightened their backs, cleared their throats and strode behind them. Cabs with horses waited to take some to nearby inns. Other guests walked to the train station. A few stayed on the pier. They all knew that people sailing to Australia usually went forever.

On board, around a dozen adult passengers remained, plus a few children. A sense of excitement began to simmer and Tom felt it too. It was a thrill, and occasional terror, to sail across the world and, even though his family now lived in America, he was glad to be heading to Melbourne again.

A tramping of footsteps clumped along the gangway onto the ship. Six black-suited Customs Officers boarded with long lists in books of who and what was supposed to be on the *Loch Ard* when she departed. They were shown about by ten crew who spent two hours with the officers, disappearing down hatches, comparing lists of crew and passengers, and inspecting all the cargo spaces.

The afternoon began to close. The winter chill crept back and people pulled collars higher. The Customs Officers closed their books and left.

Tom was grateful when supper was served. He hugged his bowl to his chest and nibbled at the hot stew. Then the newest crewman, an apprentice, dropped to sit next to him.

'I'm Rob Strasenburgh,' he said. 'But folk usually call me Straz.'

'Tom Pearce,' Tom said, blowing on his stew.

'Nice to see some young ladies on board,' Straz said.

Tom paused.

'Don't worry!' Straz said, raising a palm. 'I know the rules. We can't fraternise with the female passengers.'

'Yep,' Tom said.

'Doesn't mean we can't appreciate them though.'

Tom agreed. An interesting mix of passengers could take some of the monotony from the journey. Or it could make it worse.

CHAPTER TWO

The day before
Eva

Hooves and wheels splashed through puddles and potholes.

'You'd think,' Dr Carmichael said, 'that with this much traffic heading towards the piers, the Board of Works would keep these roads in better shape.'

He leaned a little to check for their stop.

'I see masts,' he said. 'Not far.'

Eva had watched him spend the first half of the morning pacing the hotel dining room, grumbling at his wife, barking at his children, and aggravating staff and other guests. She finally rescued them all by convincing him to take her to watch the loading of the ship.

'I hope they take care of my desk,' he said.

'Father! You put so much packing around it, they could toss it from the pier to the ship and it would bounce. Soon you'll have it unwrapped and in your cabin.'

Weeks earlier, hoping to fit his writing desk in, he had written to request the cabin measurements and the thought had upset his wife a lot.

'There'll barely be space for me to dress!' she wailed, and he told her not to fuss.

The doctor raised the cane he carried for effect and tapped it on the canopy frame.

He called out the window, 'We'll walk from here!' He helped Eva step out beside a shop then threw a coin to the driver.

Eva, 19, and her father often walked together, but the doctor refused to walk with Raby who was two years older than Eva. Raby would protest and huff about every puddle or grain of dirt. But Eva barely noticed her walking-shoes getting muddy, or the hem of her skirt becoming soggy, or if she needed to sidestep a fresh mound of horse manure.

She loved to soak in what was around her and stared, at that moment, beyond the buildings to where masts tipped back and forth and gulls cawed in overhead circles and swoops. Everywhere were the sights and sounds of animals, luggage, cargo and sailors, and a whole different life to the one at home.

At a corner, they passed a faded sign dangling from chains overhead that announced the Three Daws inn. Around the corner, on the Thames, the drawing tide made a dozen ships strain on their anchor chains. Tugs on the river smoked and chugged, and some sounded their horns.

Eva and her father halted. Twenty yards away, ropes as thick as a man's wrist tethered two huge iron ships to bollards on either side of the pier. Creaking cranes loaded cargo into one ship, and unloaded from the other. Sailors banged or scrubbed or painted. Sails draped their lashed canvas like puffy shirt sleeves.

The ship on the left pointed her bow towards shore and the one on the right pointed towards the river.

'This one,' the doctor said indicating some lettering on the ship to their right, and Eva heard quiet awe in his voice.

'So this is the *Loch Ard*,' she whispered. It was not the biggest ship on the river, but sat solidly and elegantly next to the pier with masts rising like trees through the deck and teetering against the cold sky. A small crane dangled a bundle of railway irons, tightly bound, while a dozen men on the deck tugged on ropes to tilt and steer the tracks through a hatch and down into the hold. A man stood on the steps and yelled orders that sent tea chests labelled "Salt Beef" and "Almonds & Nuts" and "Pearl Barley" and "Coffee" into another hatch.

In a corner near a deckhouse, a crewman in loose trousers and a tucked-in, once-white shirt sat cross-legged on a coil of rope stitching the hem of a crisp sail. A few feet away, a carpenter hammered short nails through a tin strip around a spar. Other sailors worked high up the masts.

At the *Loch Ard*'s rear, a separate platform sat above the main deck as though it was a slab of land forced up by an earthquake. Three men in uniforms stood there in conversation.

'Eva, see that gentleman on the right?' her father said. 'I'd say he's the captain. Let's introduce ourselves.'

He led the way up the gangway then down four steps onto the ship. The uniformed men paused their conversation.

'Good morning, sir!' Dr Carmichael called up to the shorter of the three. 'Are you the captain?'

'I am,' the man said, gliding down the steps easily and landing beside Eva. 'I'm Captain Gibb.'

'Captain, I'm Dr Evory Carmichael, your surgeon for this voyage. This is my daughter, Eveline.'

The captain nodded at Eva. 'Morning, Miss Carmichael.'

'Nice to meet you, Captain Gibb,' Eva said.

Gibb glanced away to check a screech from the cargo crane then smiled back at his guests.

'It's wonderful to meet you both,' he said, and even his eyes smiled. 'I only came on board a couple of hours ago.

Captain Johnson is in the hospital and they telegrammed me just three days ago to replace him.'

Dr Carmichael nodded. 'Captain, I'll be on board first thing tomorrow with my family, unless you have need for me today.'

Eva did not hear much more of the conversation. The ship was all voices and masts and sails. It was decks. And ladders of rope that rose up the masts like coal-stained cobwebs. It was a whole new world.

Their father was determined to stretch their minds. Just last night he sat at supper in the hotel and waited until Raby had her fork an inch from her mouth then fired an algebra question at her. It happened to all the children. Eva's younger brother Evory, who'd just turned 16, usually answered correctly. Thomas and Margaret would throw back any answer that might be close. Little Annie was more like Eva. She took her time and was usually right. But since William had left home, the doctor threw the hardest questions at Eva and Raby.

Their father stretched their minds and now he was stretching their lives. Eva could barely imagine what life would be like for them on the other side of the world.

Then, suddenly, her father was shaking hands with Captain Gibb and saying goodbye. Eva smiled at the captain who already had his attention back on his ship.

'What do you think, Father?' Eva asked, stepping off the gangway back onto the pier.

'The ship appears in good condition. As the captain said, he doesn't know all the crew yet, but he believes it's a fine company. Even so, we must remember who we are. Paying passengers must be treated with respect and it looks like Gibb's a man who understands that.'

Dr Carmichael pulled his watch from his waistcoat.

'We'll eat at that inn,' he said. Another anomaly about him. So harsh at home with all the children; so thrifty with every shilling; but, without warning, offering a treat meal with Eva. She suspected the treat was for him too – meaning they could stay away from the smothering hotel another hour.

So they turned their backs on the *Loch Ard* and strode towards the Three Daws.

CHAPTER THREE

Saturday 2 March – Gravesend
Eva

After the welcome party, Eva and Raby followed their father along the dull corridor of cabins.

'This is yours,' he said, opening a door. He stood back and let them peer in. 'Your mother and I are further along. And Margaret and Annie are sharing the half cabin beyond ours.'

Raby stepped in. She turned and her eyes met Eva's.

'Where are Evory and Thomas?' Eva asked her father.

'They're in a forward bunkroom,' he answered, 'sharing a second-class cabin with another young man.'

Another money saver, Eva thought.

'If you unpack your trunks quickly,' their father said, 'I'll send a steward to take them to the hold. It'll give you more space.' He spun and marched away.

'Three months in this,' Raby whispered. Horror shaded her face. 'I'd imagined something … grander.'

Eva peered across the top bunk. Beyond the porthole, legs walked along the pier. Soon, it would only be the ocean out there.

'Which bed should I have?' Raby asked. 'The top bed for the view, or the bottom one in case I fall off?'

'Shall we go week about?' Eva asked. 'I'll start at the top if you like.'

'Yes,' Raby said, but she was already pulling a dress from her trunk and holding it up to inspect.

A small couch was attached to the wall. Eva ran her hand over the red velvet and the gold piping then realised that the seat was hinged. She lifted it.

'There's room in here for our hat boxes and shoes,' she said to Raby.

'Thank goodness!'

They unpacked awkwardly around each other. Eva smoothed a small, crocheted blanket over the centre of her bed and propped an embroidered cushion her grandmother had given her against her pillow. Raby swirled a lace counterpane on hers. They hauled their empty trunks into the corridor then paused and looked at the space in the cabin.

'It feels a little more like home now,' Raby said, but her voice lacked cheer.

The gonging of the bell trailed down the companionway steps and into the corridor.

'Perhaps they're casting off?' Eva said. In the passageway, they hastily examined the brass oval tokens on the doors until they found the privy then took turns to use it before they went up.

In the river, two tugs lingered near the bow, puffing smoke from their throbbing engines. Dockworkers prepared to cast off the ropes from the bollards.

While Raby wandered to the starboard side, Eva moved to the rail nearest the pier and pushed in between her brothers. She was wearing her favourite blue dress but now the breeze chilled her and she wished she'd grabbed her shawl.

Thomas leaned out, then squinted up, then hovered forward, then looked back across the deck.

'Thomas! Can't you stand still?' Eva said, glaring at him.

Thomas grinned at her. The sky danced in his eyes.

'One of the sailors said he'd teach me how to work the sails!'

'Why?' Evory grumbled. 'Don't be stupid Thomas! You'd better not let Father see you trying to be a sailor. You know how he was about William.'

'Father'll be too busy looking after seasick passengers,' Thomas said cheerfully. 'I'm off to watch the tugs.' And he hurried away.

William was the eldest and his father had insisted he study to become a doctor, but when he was seventeen William disappeared. A letter arrived a week later and delivered relief to them all, and then anger and sadness because William had run away to sea. Since then, their father almost never mentioned him, and the rest of the children only spoke about him in whispers. William had written two or three times each year and a letter had come at Christmas saying he was working in Melbourne.

'Oh, we'll see him when we land!' Mrs Carmichael had said with delight.

Eva gazed at the river full of ships, row boats and tugs. No more planning. No more Ireland. No more looking back. They were leaving for a new life. She swallowed a lump in her throat and looked down as the space between the *Loch Ard* and the pier expanded to feet then yards. Some passengers waved to the few still watching, but there was no one waving to the Carmichaels from Cork.

'Eva!' She turned to see her mother teetering towards her, gripping the hands of the two youngest girls.

'Annie's just had one of her little turns,' Mrs Carmichael said.

Annie's brown eyes had that loose, floating look they got just after a fit, and her face was pale. On the other side of their mother, Margaret was tugging as hard as she could.

'Mama, let me go. I want to see the sailboats!'

'Mother,' Eva said. 'I'll take Margaret to watch from up on that back deck.'

'Thomas said that's called the poop deck,' Margaret said, and giggled. She snatched at Eva's hand.

'Is it really?' Eva asked her mother.

But Mrs Carmichael was already swaying towards the companionway steps, dragging Annie behind her.

'Margaret,' Eva said. 'Do you know where Father is?'

Margaret shrugged. 'I saw him being cross with one of the sailors.'

'Oh dear.'

Their father had applied for the position of ship's doctor for this voyage, and it would save most of his fare, which had cheered him. But they were all now on a ship together with no rest from one another. Eva could no longer roam through the meadows to clear her head, or go window shopping in town with Raby, or visit with friends or cousins. She looked around at the crew and wondered which one had promised to teach Thomas to sail.

Whoever he was, he'd better not have need of the doctor.

CHAPTER FOUR

Tom

'You're Pearce?'

Tom spun away from coiling a rope and found himself face to face with the new captain.

'Aye, Captain Gibb. Yes sir!' he said. He groaned inside. This was their introduction and Gibb's eyes were already raking through Tom's bruises and swollen purple eye socket.

'Mac told me you were robbed in London.'

'Yes, sir.' It had been a stupid mistake. A dark alley. Not paying attention.

'And he's assured me you're not a troublemaker.' Gibb glanced over his shoulder. They'd be casting off soon.

'Not at all, sir. I won't give you a minute's bother,' Tom said.

'Good.' Gibb shoved his hands into his jacket pockets. He frowned. 'So, what's that accent Pearce?'

'Australian, sir. I'm from Melbourne.'

Gibb nodded.

'And a question I ask all my apprentices: Why did you sign up?'

Pearce had signed up for his apprenticeship two years earlier. But why? It all got lost in the fact that the ocean refused to leave his mind.

As a child, Tom had found a book about seamanship that he poured over every single day. The ocean took root inside him. Then his father died and his mother married a sea captain. Then, less than a year later, the sea captain drowned in a shipwreck. Even so, the ocean still called him. Finally, Tom sailed to London and signed up for an apprenticeship and worked hard for the day he'd master his own ship and sail people and cargo across the world.

Before he could answer the captain's question, a passenger tapped him on the shoulder and Gibb whirled around to a youngish man about Tom's height with a lank composure and a premature hint of a stoop.

'Good afternoon. You're Mr … Jones?' Gibb guessed.

'Yes sir, Reginald Jones.' He fidgeted with two rings on his middle finger – a silver signet ring and a thin gold band. 'Captain Gibb, I need to tell you I've never sailed before. And … this voyage terrifies me.'

Jones' eyes flitted to Tom and back to the captain. His voice tremored. 'Do you promise we'll be safe?'

'Of course we'll be safe Mr Jones.' Gibb's words came out clipped.

'It's just,' Jones went on, 'I read somewhere that this very ship lost all her masts barely five years ago – on a voyage like this … to Australia.'

The captain hesitated before he answered and Tom wondered if he knew anything about the *Loch Ard*.

'That's correct,' Gibb said, surprising Tom. 'But, Mr Jones, major improvements were made during the repairs in Australia. They installed far better masts and rigging and since then the *Loch Ard* has voyaged this route several times.' He paused and squared up to Jones. 'So, I need to insist you keep your anxieties to yourself or you'll upset the other passengers. If you're worried about anything, come to me and we'll talk about it.'

Jones stared at the river beyond Gibb's shoulder then sighed, almost rudely.

'I'll try,' he said. 'But, Captain, have you even sailed this route?'

Gibb inhaled fully, maybe to stop himself punching Jones. 'No. This is my first voyage to Australia but our first-mate knows the route and the waters well.' Then he gestured towards Tom. 'And Pearce here is from Melbourne. Right Pearce?'

Tom stepped into the conversation. 'Yes, Captain,' he said, then he looked directly into Jones's watery eyes. 'I've been on this ship nearly two years Mr Jones. When we docked here a couple of weeks ago, it was after an easy voyage from Melbourne. You can ask any of us how the *Loch Ard* performs. She's a gem!' Jones eyes traced Tom's battered face.

Gibb nodded. 'You see, Mr Jones, you're in good hands on a proven ship. You must relax. Three months is a long time if you're nervous, and even longer if you spread it around. Once we've been at sea a few days, you'll find we know what we're doing.'

Jones surrendered, nodded and backed clumsily against the cages that held the chickens and half a dozen bleating spring lambs that would each take their turn during the voyage to be roasted in the galley oven. Jones looked like he was about to bleat too.

'Captain!' Mac called. 'Ready to depart, sir.'

Gibb nodded at Mac. He looked at Tom. 'We'll finish our conversation later.' He began to move away then pivoted back.

'Pearce,' he said in a low voice. 'Keep an eye on Jones.'

'Aye, sir.'

Tom had seen passengers with Jones's affliction before. They'd often combed too many newspapers – stories of wrecks and careless crews. Then they arrived on board after too many sleepless nights. They were edgy, usually alone, and almost always ill with fear before the ship even cast off.

The chugging grew louder. The men on the tugs were stoking fires to hold the engines at full strength. Smoke poured from the funnels. The tugs were preparing to guide the *Loch Ard* east along the Thames to anchor for a few hours before she would be set free to the ocean.

Three months without touching land.

Tom's bunkroom was one of four identical cramped bunkrooms in the deckhouse forward on the main deck, all under a single roof. Seven other men shared Tom's bunkroom, including Straz.

That night Tom lay on his top bunk knowing he'd sleep better than Jones would. He grinned, punched his pillow into a softer ball, and fell soundly asleep.

CHAPTER FIVE

Sunday 3 March
89 days to Melbourne
Tom

Tom stood far forward watching the water surge out in loud, steely waves from the ship's bow below him. Eight miles to his right, the eastern corner of England was already fading. Overhead, several sails were popping. The deck heaved in its familiar swell under his feet and the joy of being back at sea washed through him. Then his belly growled for breakfast.

During the night, the *Loch Ard* had moved along the Thames and into the English Channel and now the chilly dawn sunlight lit the sails and turned curves of canvas into gold. Mac bellowed an order from the poop deck, and the ship tilted a slow lean to starboard and began to ease west along the Strait of Dover between the coasts of England and France.

Passengers began to rise through the companionways. They gazed at the land and the water and the crew and the sails. One passenger, Mr Stuckey, staggered to the port rail and vomited into the sea.

When breakfast was done, Tom sat near the deckhouse and polished his boots. The pilot needed to be rowed ashore to the Isle of Wight so Mac ordered reduced sails, then sent men to the davits to lower a boat.

'Hello Tom!' Thomas Carmichael bounced in front of him. Right behind him hovered a serious boy.

'Morning Thomas,' Tom said.

'This is my brother, Evory Junior.'

'Just Evory,' the brother snapped. 'I've told you before, they call Father "Doctor", which means no one needs to call me Junior.' Evory ignored Tom. A book was wedged under his arm. 'You know that Father will get properly heated if he sees you doing sailor work.'

Thomas shrugged and his eyes swept across the deck and up the masts, absorbing the whole ship in a moment.

'You go and read if you want,' he said. 'I'm going to learn to sail.'

'Whatever,' Evory mumbled.

'What's the book, Evory?' Tom asked before Evory could move away.

Tom generally only read books for his apprenticeship – books on ropes, navigation, signal flags, sails, shipping rules, ship structure, discipline.

Evory flashed the spine towards Tom, as though testing if a mere sailor could read.

'*Twenty Thousand Leagues Under the Sea*,' Tom said. 'An interesting one to have on a voyage.'

Evory's face shadowed. 'It was better in French. The translator ruined it.'

'So why are you reading it?' Tom asked before wondering if he should.

'I'm noting all the mistakes so I can translate it myself when we reach Australia.' He turned his back on them and made a path towards the stern and it occurred to Tom it would be helpful if Reg Jones did not get a glimpse of *Twenty Thousand Leagues Under the Sea*.

'Righto,' he said to Thomas as he pulled on his boots. 'Stick near me and I'll explain as I go. But if I'm sent up a mast, you'll have to stay on the deck.'

Gloom swept Thomas's face.

'For now, at least,' Tom said. 'I need to know you'll follow orders before I take you onto the shrouds and ratlines.'

'Oh, right,' Thomas said. His face brightened. 'I definitely can follow orders!'

'First,' Tom said, 'I'll teach you how we hitch the lines to the pinrails.' He led Thomas along the curtainlike row of ropes leading down from the spars to wooden pins along the side. He chose a rope, released it from the pinrail and demonstrated the knot to lash it back again. Thomas fumbled once, almost got it, then finally produced a firm knot on his third attempt.

'Not bad,' Tom said. 'This rope is usually a spare. You can practice whenever you like on this pinrail, but always check up to where the line leads in case it's in use.'

Thomas nodded. 'I was wondering …' He looked at Tom, hesitant. 'How'd you get those bruises?'

Tom's fingers rose to his black eye. Most of the ache had gone from it.

'I got robbed in London.'

'Ouch,' Thomas said.

'Could have been worse.' Tom led the way back towards midships. He spotted Evory sitting on the main deck with his back against the warm galley wall. On his lap was his book. In his hand was a pencil.

'Are your family sailors then?' Thomas asked.

'Mostly not.'

'So why are you?'

Tom paused.

'I guess I feel like it's my place in the world,' he said. 'I can't imagine doing anything else.' He pressed a hand to the thick wood of the mainmast. 'Being on the sea is my place. Most of the year, a ship's not tied to anything, which means my place in the world is not tied either. Does that make sense?'

Thomas put his hand on the mast too and seemed to be sensing something deep, from far below the ship. 'Yes, it actually does.'

Mac yelled, 'All hands! Heave to!'

'That means the full crew,' Tom said. 'Stay here and watch.'

He joined a dozen men taking in the sails to slow the *Loch Ard*. Four men and the channel pilot climbed into the longboat then a dozen sailors lowered it over the side.

The *Loch Ard* waited, the crew in position, for over an hour until the longboat returned and was raised and lashed.

Orders were called. Ropes were hauled. Sails snapped full, and the *Loch Ard* crept up to five then seven knots. Tom slithered back down to the deck. He beckoned Thomas to help tie off a line.

'That was fantastic!' Thomas said. The bell rang for the church service. 'Can I find you later? Or tomorrow?' he asked.

'Whenever you like.'

Captains encouraged their crew to host the passengers whenever they could. Happy passengers meant a good report at the end of the trip and more ticket sales for the future. Usually the boys who showed excitement at the beginning got bored in the first few days.

Most of the fifty souls on the *Loch Ard* piled in a jovial group about the main deck and Gibb led them all in a hymn, accompanied only by a crewman's tin whistle, and then Gibb read from his service book. When it was over and the passengers had scattered, he looked around dissatisfied then ordered to the second-mate to make a note for the following week that there should be seats for the ladies, and for the piano to be brought up any Sunday the weather allowed.

Tom saw Reg Jones release his hold on the main mast and creep through midships in an attempt to corner the captain. But Mac spotted him too and cut him off before he could get there. He dropped his big hand on the man's shoulder.

'Come on Mr Jones,' Mac said. 'Come aft and join us fishing! There'll be several of the crew, and a few passengers up there too.'

A flock of gulls screeched and swooped through the clipper's path.

Jones shrank his head down and escaped Mac's arm.

'No thank you,' he said and he fled to the companionway steps that led down to the cabins.

'One on every trip,' Tom muttered.

A cool breeze whistled across the deck, and the coast of France scoured the southern horizon. To the north, England was slipping away and had become a faint smudge. A few passengers stood at the rail watching it disappear.

'I'll get you!' a child squealed and Tom only just jumped out of the way before the two youngest Carmichael girls chased past him. Their mother, up on the poop deck, seemed to be more interested in a deep conversation with Mrs Stuckey than in watching her children.

Mac, red-faced, strode into the path of the girls while they were on their second lap of the deck.

'Stop!' he bellowed. The girls halted, panting. Mac glared at them.

'Children are not to run on the deck!' he grumbled. 'Do you understand?'

Both girls stared up as though Mac was a tower. They nodded. Mac strode away and the girls giggled into cupped hands and danced away towards their mother.

A waft of coffee filtered from the galley and Tom went to his bunkroom to fetch his mug.

Straz was beside his bunk and jolted in surprise. He flicked his blanket over a small canvas bag.

'Ah.' His face flushed. 'Hello Tom.'

'Straz,' Tom said, grabbing his mug. 'Everything alright?'

'Sure is,' Straz said. He turned and leaned his shoulders back on the bunk frame and shoved his hands into his pockets.

'So, what was Mac yelling about?'

'It was those two young girls,' Tom said. 'They run everywhere.'

'I've a couple'a sisters,' said Straz. 'I never understand girls.'

Tom nodded. He had sisters too. He and Straz were about the same age. Both apprentices. And both usually given the dodgy jobs on board.

'Same,' Tom said. He glanced at the lump under the blanket then took his mug and headed to the galley where he poured hot coffee from the pot. As he sipped and let the liquid warm his insides, he spotted Straz step out of the bunkroom with the bag held against his belly. Tom leaned out to see forward along the deck to where Straz was going. Straz walked past a couple of passengers in their deck chairs smoking pipes and reading their newspapers of already-old news.

'Watch out!' Billy Johnson, the cook's mate, yelled. He pushed past dangling four lanterns.

'Sorry Billy.' By the time Billy had hung a lantern on the hook beside the galley and stepped aside, Straz had vanished.

That night Tom lay uneasily in bed. His head was less than two feet from Straz's in the next bunk. He sensed trouble and woke half-a-dozen times before the bell rang for his pre-dawn watch.

CHAPTER SIX

Off the west coast of Portugal
Tom

Tom's diary: "A week out from England on the *Loch Ard* again and everything feels different. The *Loch Ard* that sailed into the Thames had a disorganised and sick captain, and two passengers prone to drunkenness and rowdiness who the officers could not control. The *Loch Ard* I've been on over the first week of the voyage has a captain who is talking well with each crewman and each passenger, and even the children.

"Weather has been fair. Wind favourable although we had to tack hard to get around Spain."

On Saturday night, after a long day of rough sea and more work than usual for the crew, Tom clambered exhausted into his bunk. He fell asleep as he lowered his head.

An hour later he was awake and pressing his pillow over his ears. Men were yelling at Billy to get out. Billy was alternating between sleeping, vomiting into a bucket, and staggering out, groaning and folded in half, to the crew privy, then returning just in time to vomit into the bucket again. When Billy could take a breath, he cursed the leftover stew he'd helped himself to, which he moaned he should have tossed to the chickens instead.

When the ship's bell rang at midnight, the crewmen on the next watch were happy to escape, even with a storm blowing in. Billy fled again and this time did not come back.

Tom managed to sleep a few more patches through the increasing heaving of the *Loch Ard* until thunder boomed in the west and lightning flashed yellow onto the small, thick panes of glass on the bunkroom's portholes. Rain drummed the roof above his head.

Then Mac crashed through the door and Tom jolted up so fast he hit his head on the ceiling. Mac's lantern illuminated the cascade of rain flooding from his hat and coat onto the bunkroom floor.

'Pearce! Giles needs you in the galley. Go fill in for Billy.' The door slammed shut.

Tom rubbed his forehead and groaned. He did not want to be cook's-mate for the day. He pulled on boots, jacket and hat. When he stepped out, the rain was easing and a grey sky had begun to brim the eastern horizon. Nearly dawn. He was almost at the galley when Giles leaned out and pointed with a carving knife to a suspended sail.

'Get that water into the barrel, then get back in here!' A sail had been tied to capture rainwater during the storm. Tom funnelled it into one of the barrels lashed to the masts. As he helped Giles in the galley, he was grateful to see the sky lighten outside and feel the wind and rain ease.

He was slicing loaves of bread when he spotted a couple of crewmen lashing a small piano to the deck and was reminded it was Sunday. At mid-morning, he was finally eating his breakfast when the bell rang. Captain Gibb waited until everyone was assembled then thanked Mrs Carmichael for volunteering to play the hymns. The piano kept them all in tune and so, as the storm became a shadow on the edge of the sky, the choir of passengers and crew treated the ocean to a short but rousing performance.

Tom and Giles spent the rest of the morning peeling and chopping seven pounds of onions into quarters for the pot, then another seven pounds into slices for the next day's soup and stew.

At midday, Giles sent Tom on trip after trip to the first-class dining pantry carrying various trays for lunch. One tray held roasted mutton and roasted potatoes, another green peas and gravy. Another rhubarb tart and custard. Then he carried two fresh pots of coffee for the stewards to keep hot to serve after lunch. And at last he and Giles finally served boiled beef and gravy rice for the crew, including themselves, and for the remaining passengers. Tom scrubbed the pots and ladles and mixing bowls, then restacked everything in the impossibly tiny spaces in the galley.

When Giles finally released him, Tom collapsed outside onto a damp coil of rope. The sun was trying to shine through the patchy clouds and the last of the rain had evaporated from the decking. He leaned back and closed his eyes for a few minutes, but it was impossible to sleep on the noisy deck. He sat up and gazed lazily around.

Two female passengers had found sheltered places to sew, and two male passengers were playing chess near the wheelhouse. On the lower rigging of the main mast, Thomas Carmichael was trying to show his older brother Evory the way Tom had taught him to climb the shrouds. And Evory was hanging on so tight that even from the deck Tom could see his tense, whitened hands. But Thomas, all lithe and wiry, flashed past him up the shrouds to the topsail yard. Evory gave up and clambered sullenly back to the deck.

Then the breeze gusted and the first-mate yelled an order for the mainsail to be set and the spanker hauled out.

Straz and three other men flew up the shrouds like ants on a cake, and stepped easily along the ratlines. Others hauled on ropes from the deck amidships. Thomas Carmichael stayed up the mast and helped with the sails.

'This one might just work out,' Tom said to himself.

The bell rang for the change of watch and put Tom back on duty. He was tying a line when Mac called him. 'Pearce! Get up the foremast and untangle that pulley!'

'Aye, sir!'

Tom clambered up the twenty feet to the jammed pulley, loosened the knot and freed the line. He turned to climb down but then something on the deck caught his eye.

Below, Straz was heading forward with his canvas bag held tight again. Without even looking around, he crept into a foredeck hatch that led towards the cargo area near the crew privy. There was nothing unusual about going to the privy but a lot unusual about the way Straz was sneaking about with that bag.

For the rest of the day, Tom could not shake a disturbance growing inside him.

'Good morning, Miss,' Tom said to one of the women passengers. She was one of the Carmichael daughters. He was edging past her to try and get to his breakfast.

'Oh, good morning Mr …?'

'Pearce. I'm Tom Pearce.'

'Good morning Mr Pearce. I'm Eva Carmichael. I believe you're the brave young man teaching my brother about sailing?'

'You mean Thomas?' Tom asked.

'Yes.'

'Why brave?'

Eva smiled a simple smile, yet Tom thought it was the probably the most honest smile he had ever seen.

'Our father would not approve.'

Tom recalled Evory's early comment about their father and he found it annoying because most parents appreciated when crew kept their offspring entertained.

'Don't let it worry you, Mr Pearce,' Eva said. Something about her made Tom relax. He nodded at her and grinned.

'I won't. Have a good day, Miss Eva.'

Mid-morning, Second-Mate Baxter yelled out, 'Square the main!'

Tom, Straz and six other crewmen teamed up on the deck to haul on the port stays to turn a yard arm to the wind. A hen clucked proudly from the coop, bragging about a new egg, and Tom and Straz glanced at her. Their eyes met and Tom figured it was now or never. For a brief moment he studied the green kerchief that was always knotted on Straz's neck. He waited a few seconds until the other men had moved away.

'Straz,' Tom said. 'I keep seeing you sneaking around with your bag. I'm not sure what's going on, but if Captain Gibb finds out there's some sort of racket aboard, he could order you caned.'

Straz was taller than Tom by about four inches and pulled himself to his full height.

'Not your business,' he growled. 'Don't you dare say a word.' Sweat popped onto his top lip. His nostrils flared.

'Alright,' Tom said. He held up a hand and leaned back a little. 'Just be careful.'

'Stop wasting time, you two!' Baxter bellowed. 'Get to the foremast, Strasenburgh.'

Without moving his eyes from Tom's, Straz yelled, 'Aye, sir!' Then words came out between his teeth, 'Leave me alone, right?'

He stowed the coil of rope and strode to the foremast.

CHAPTER SEVEN

Tom

When Tom Pearce was two years old, he was the youngest of three children and his name was Tom Millett. His father was a civil engineer and surveyor, and he had just moved the family to Kilmore in Victoria to start a new job surveying the district.

They lived in a large government house with two storeys of stone and oak, and a forbidden attic in the roof. The attic held the belongings of another family who had been sent on contract to Queensland and who would return one day.

The house was cool in summer and freezing in winter. Tom's mother, Emily, spent all her time profoundly busy with the house, growing vegetables, and cooking for the family of five. When Tom's older sisters were not at school, they took him on ramblings about the house and the large, tree-filled garden.

One day when Tom was four, he dragged six-year-old Mary to the upstairs landing. He stopped at the bottom of the cramped steps that led to the forbidden attic. He had timed this outing for when their mother was at the end of the garden watering peas and beans and figured he had about the time of two bedtime stories for a hasty examination of the forbidden attic.

'Stay here Mary,' he said in his father's tone but his little-boy voice. 'Keep watch and I'll bring you a treasure.' Mary had not grown as fast as Tom, and folk often mistook them for twins. Tom grasped her shoulders and pressed her down until she was sitting on the bottom step.

'Are you alright?'

Mary nodded. She had come against her will and she hugged her rag doll.

There was no time for creeping and Tom sped up the narrow steps. He stood on tiptoes, reached high, and turned the door handle. Nothing happened. He twisted the handle the other way and the door squeaked open. Copper-coloured light trickled in around curtained dormer windows, but this first moment of motion after two years of peace caused dust on nearby boxes and rolled rugs and tea chests to puff, and the first noise Tom Millett made on this secret mission was a huge sneeze.

He had to find treasure for Mary, and for himself, fast. In the middle of the attic stood some piles of books. He grabbed a brown, cloth-bound book with an embossed dusty title and a sailing ship on the cover. His heart pounded. He brushed the dust away and stuffed the book under his arm. For a minute or two he marched bravely in little-boy strides around the attic. Nothing.

His search for another treasure exploded into a growing panic. Then, on a tea chest under the furthest part of the eave was a wooden bowl covered with a lace of cobwebs. His fingers broke through and he pulled out one of perhaps two dozen large gumnuts, all decorated by forgotten children. Buttons for eyes, chopped red pipe-cleaner for the mouth, and a piece of wire through the top for hanging. Decorations?

He shoved the gumnut into his shorts pocket and fled.

Every day for months, Tom pulled the book he had stolen from the attic out of the bottom of his toy chest. And every time, he began again at the first page. Most of the words were beyond him but the images of cross-sections of ships, rigging, knots, flags, compasses and route maps all carved themselves into his mind. One day, he finally sounded out one word on the cover – "Sea-man-ship". Then a few months later he pieced the title together – "The-ory and Prac-tice of Sea-man-ship".

The Milletts lived inland, but everything in the book made him think of the ocean.

When he was six, the family moved back to Melbourne and Tom spent hours every week with his mates on a jetty at the edge of the River Yarra determined to learn to swim. Even in winter they wore woollen jumpers and challenged each other to dives and backward somersaults from the jetty.

Tom was fourteen when his father died.

His mother remarried and her new husband was Captain Robert Pearce. His mother changed Tom and the other children's names to Pearce, and, through his new father, ships came even more alive for Tom.

When he turned fifteen, he sailed to London and signed up to the merchant navy and stepped aboard the real world of his dreams.

CHAPTER EIGHT

Tuesday 12 March
200 miles northwest of Morocco
80 days to Melbourne
Eva

Eva adapted to ship life faster than Raby who often rose from bed late and arrived at breakfast grumpy. No servants were here for the Carmichaels and even the first-class passengers had a routine they were expected to follow.

A month before they left Cork, Eva's father spent two-pence on a handbook called '*Out At Sea*'. It listed the same rules Captain Gibb had read to them all from the poop deck. The rules stated that every day the passengers and crew must sweep out their cabins. And when the weather was dry, passengers and crew must wash their clothes and hang them to dry on lines around the deck. And every week all mattresses must be flipped and left to air with the blankets for a few hours, and all sheets must be washed.

Eva sat beside Raby that evening at supper. The day had been a long day of the Carmichaels wiping and sweeping out their cabins, washing and drying bedding, and remaking their beds. Even their father had needed to help his wife fight with the sheets that had dried fast on the lines amidships. Captain Gibb was with the first-class passengers for supper too. And it seemed to Eva that her father waited until everyone was eating before he addressed the captain.

He cleared his throat. 'Captain Gibb. Can you tell me why everyone, including those in first-class, must follow all these extravagant rules for cleaning, and routines, and mealtimes?'

The captain swallowed his food. He lowered his cutlery but kept his grip on them. Tighter than needed, Eva noticed. His eyes swept the others then circled back to the doctor.

'That's a fair question Dr Carmichael. The main reason is for health, of course. It's too easy for vermin and pests to settle in and breed, and there's all the usual problems that can arise, like lice.'

The doctor nodded his agreement and began to part his lips to respond.

'But,' Gibb said quickly, 'these voyages are long and each man of my crew is rostered to work a minimum of twelve hours a day. They must look after their own bedding and cleaning, and the washing and mending of their own clothes. If I hired extra crew to look after passengers' cabins, we'd have to carry less cargo so we could accommodate them. I'd have to feed and pay them too. The price of everyone's ticket would be increased to cover the extra crew and the lack of a full hold of cargo.'

Eva felt her face get hot and she saw her father's did also, flashing pink for a few seconds.

Around the room, heads agreed, cautiously. Eyes flitted to the doctor then back to their supper.

'And,' Gibb added, 'with all of us confined to the small dimensions of this ship, it's good to have routine, including simple expectations on everyone. Even the children.'

After some long seconds of silence, Dr Carmichael said, 'I understand, Captain. Thank you.' He picked up his cutlery then cut a little too firmly into a piece of potato, which shot off his plate and landed in damp thud on the floor. He left it there.

The next afternoon, Eva and her mother were lazing on deck chairs on the main deck. Eva was trying to concentrate on a book her cousin had given her called *The Turn of the Screw*. Her mother flicked slowly through a dress catalogue. It was restful in the intermittent sunlight.

Then, from above them, a howl filled the air. A metal bucket crashed against the galley stovepipe before clattering onto the deck just a few feet from Eva's chair. The bucket rolled sticky black tar in arcs across the deck.

'I can't … hold!' a man cried.

Twenty feet above, a sailor swung by his hands from a spar. Half a dozen crewmen rushed towards the main mast.

'Mother,' Eva exclaimed. 'He's going to fall!'

They leapt up and backed away from their chairs.

'Hold on!' voices shouted. 'We're coming!'

Then Eva's mother groaned.

'Thomas!' she wailed. 'No!' She snatched blindly at Eva's sleeve.

From above the dangling sailor, their Thomas slid down a rope and landed lightly astride the spar where the man hung. He fell forward onto his chest and shot one hand either side of the spar and seized the man's left arm. Several long seconds later two more sailors arrived. One spun down under the spar and whirled a rope around the sailor's chest just as the sailor lost his grip.

The sudden heaviness of the man snatched Thomas sideways, but he kept his hold until the man was secured.

'Let go,' someone said, and Thomas released the man's arm and sat upright.

'Lower him down,' yelled the second-mate from the poop deck. Everyone's eyes were focused up.

Mrs Carmichael whispered beside Eva. 'My … Thomas.'

'What is this?' Eva's father roared. His head appeared up the companionway steps and he marched past Eva, glaring up the mast at his youngest son. He shaded his eyes with a hand and an ugly line of purple crept up his neck and into his jaw.

'Thomas Joseph Carmichael!' he barked. Eva could tell that Thomas had heard because he flinched, then turned his head away and deliberately looked across the ocean at the horizon.

'Oh no!' Eva whispered.

'Evory dear, it's alright!' Mrs Carmichael said, but her husband ignored her.

Then Captain Gibb appeared beside them.

'Doctor,' Gibb said. He stepped right around in front of the doctor and looked directly at him.

'Captain!' Dr Carmichael dragged his eyes away from his son. His cold word came out in a snap that seemed to suck the oxygen from the air around him. 'Tell me, sir! Why are your men tempting my son to play games up there?'

Gibb propped his smoking pipe in the air an inch from his lips. There was a glint in his eye and briefly he cast Eva a calming look.

'You misunderstand, Doctor. See that man being lowered on that rope? Well, your son just saved his life.'

Dr Carmichael noticed, for the first time, the man dangling below his son.

'So, Dr Carmichael,' Gibb said. 'I'll be writing this into the ship's log as a permanent record. Your Thomas reached young Magnus Murray before my men could get there. Seems he's a bit of a natural sailor, and very brave.'

Eva watched the purple begin to recede down her father's neck and turn a soft pink.

'Oh. I misunderstood.' He glanced up again. 'Thank you, Captain. It's just that I don't like my son … I had hoped …'

'I know, I know.' Gibb reached out and shook the doctor's hand. 'All I'm saying is that your Thomas has shown his skill and bravery. We're all very grateful to him.'

Gibb drew on his pipe then puffed out a slow ring of smoke.

'Now, Doctor, could I ask you to check on Murray please? A rope around my chest once broke one of my ribs. I'd appreciate your professional judgement.' He pointed his pipe towards the forward companionway. 'I'll have the men take him to the sickbay.'

The doctor seemed to shrink a little. 'Of course, Captain. I'll fetch my bag.' He glanced at his wife and daughter and left.

Eva's heart was pounding. Captain Gibb seemed to understand all people, even her father.

Thomas descended the mast while the men helped lay out the crewman and others began the tedious task of scraping spilt tar off the galley stovepipe and deck.

Her mother eased herself back onto her chair and smoothed out the wrinkles on her catalogue. Her hands shook very slightly.

Eva was twelve when she first saw a dead body. Her father's surgery was attached to their house and Eva had thought her father had gone out so had stepped into his office. But Dr Carmichael was on the floor trying to resuscitate a woman who had just had a heart attack. The woman's husband was standing there, white as ivory. No one had seen Eva come in. She crept out and ran through their back garden and vomited behind the rose bushes, and her whole body had shivered for hours afterwards.

Eva sat back and gripped her closed book. Despite the sunshine, her skin had become cold and clammy.

'Are you alright, dear?' her mother asked, half looking at her.

'Just a chill, Mother.' Eva stood, aware that her legs were like jelly. 'I'll go for my shawl. Do you need anything while I'm down there?'

'Yes. Please see if the girls have finished tidying their cabin. If they have, they may come up and play.'

Eva went to the girls' cabin and helped them hang a couple of dresses on hangers and put away their dolls' clothes, then released them up to the deck. Inside her own cabin, she wrapped her warmest shawl around her shoulders, then sank onto the couch and tipped her head back against the wall.

She had nearly seen a man die.

'It's nothing,' she said to herself. 'Just a bit of shock.' And she decided that this doctor's daughter needed to toughen up. She took a few deep breaths and went to sit back with her mother.

CHAPTER NINE

Wednesday 13 March
200 miles northwest of Morocco
79 days to Melbourne
Tom

Tom and two other men balanced on the bowsprit struggling to haul in the flying jib. Twenty minutes earlier, just after dawn, they'd heard a wall of wind approaching. It was like the sound of a train thundering in fast. The surface of the ocean that had been a swelling surface of lapping waves was now an angry, choppy mess of waves and spray.

The bowsprit was the most exposed part of the ship. The long prong pointed forward over the water. When the ocean was rough and sailors were out on it, the ship often dipped so far forward that the sea would lick their boots. When things weren't as rushed as at that moment, Tom found it exciting being there at the front of the ship especially when it raced sometimes at eleven or twelve knots, and having the spray sting his face, and salt stick to his lips.

'Come on! Get that canvas in!' the second-mate, Baxter, bellowed.

Then Baxter yelled again. 'Strasenburgh! Pearce! Get up the foremast and fix that line before we lose it!'

'Aye, sir!'

Up the rigging, he and Straz tied off the line. The sail it was attached to snapped full of wind again and Tom began to move back along the ratline to the shroud. Below, he spotted the captain speaking with Baxter. Baxter nodded then looked around the deck.

'You three!' he yelled at three men landing on the deck from the poop.

'Aye, sir,' one called back.

'Weather's going to be too bad for a few days now. Fetch your tools and go batten down all the hatches.'

Beside Tom, Straz stopped dead.

'No,' he said. 'They can't.'

Tom hung onto the yard arm. Straz's face had turned white.

'What's wrong?' Tom asked.

'I … They can't.' Straz began to climb down then stopped. He was breathing hard. He stared blankly across the sea.

'Straz, tell me!' Tom demanded.

Straz paused. He glanced up at Tom and his eyes were wide.

'Tom, you gotta help me.' He looked down at the deck where the men were carrying hammers, nail and battens. He pressed his forehead to the mast.

Tom's heart was thumping now. 'What?'

Straz seemed to have lost all strength, which was deadly high up in the whistling rigging. The wind whipped at ropes and canvases and at their clothes and hair.

Straz shook his head slowly. 'You were right when you saw me, before. It's turned out much harder than I'd thought.' He looked down. 'Impossible now.'

'What has?' Tom asked.

'What's going on up there?' Baxter yelled.

'Coming sir!' Tom called back.

Straz looked at Tom. 'Meet me at noon when we get off watch. Behind the galley.'

Tom sensed trouble, and trouble was the thing he'd promised Gibb he'd stay out of.

When the lunch bell rang, Tom collected his bowl of hot mutton slices, steaming roasted onion, and buttered bread. He filled his mug with ale then stumbled on the rolling deck until he got to the back of the galley. Straz was tucked into the corner picking at his bread. His canvas bag was bundled on the floor under his leg and only a sliver of meat was left in his bowl. He must be a fast eater.

Off to the west, a line of lightning flashed. Spray blew across the deck. Straz finished his ale then chocked his empty mug against his thigh. He looked behind him, took a deep breath then leaned towards Tom.

'Tom,' he said slowly. 'I've brought someone on board.'

Tom's first response was to look around too, but then it hit him.

'No, Straz.' Horror crept through him. 'Not a stowaway?'

Straz held up his palm. 'Not so loud,' he said. 'It's a long story.'

Tom's eyes fell on the canvas bag. 'And you've been sharing your food with him. Or her? And starving yourself?'

'Him,' Straz said. He wiped his mouth with a corner of his kerchief. 'It's Jimmy, my cousin. He was a stable hand and the manager promised to train him as a jockey. But the man kept beating Jimmy and never gave him proper pay or any training.' Straz's eyes swept over the tumbling ocean and then back to Tom. 'Anyway, I got him on board when all the visitors were here – before we left. Snuck him into the forward cargo hold. I've been moving him around a bit, and today he's in the storage area under the forward hatch.

'And everything's been battened down.'

'Somehow, I've gotta get him out,' Straz said.

It would be difficult to move a stranger around the ship. Impossible actually.

'I had no idea how hard it'd be.' His hand touched the canvas bag. 'I keep saving any food I can, then I get it to Jimmy every day or so, but,' and his face tightened, 'I can't even do that now.'

'Straz, we still have more than ten weeks at sea,' Tom said. 'He'll die if he's stuck there for even a few days.'

Straz didn't move.

'We have to tell the captain!' But Straz just sat and stared at the deck, until a wave struck side-on and sprayed them both.

'I can't.' His eyes trailed. 'Maybe tonight I can find a way to loosen the battens, so I can get food and water to him?'

It'd be as easy as trying to pull hairs from a pig's tail.

'You could help,' Straz added weakly.

Do what? Wander about with a hammer and crowbar then prise open the hatch? With men on watch?

'Straz,' Tom said. 'I'll bet we're far enough out now that Captain Gibb won't put your cousin ashore anywhere.'

Straz's shoulders slumped. 'And what would happen to me?'

'I'm not sure. I barely know Gibb,' Tom said. Gibb seemed to be a by-the-rules man. 'But I'll come with you. We should go right now.'

Straz shook his head.

Tom shoved his bowl onto the deck. 'Straz! There's no other way. Think about it! You've hit a wall with this.'

Straz stood and gripped the edge of the galley roof. He turned his face to the wind. Finally, he looked down at Tom.

'Alright. But I'd better put this in my bunk,' he said, holding up the bag.

CHAPTER TEN

Tom

In the narrow corridor that led to the captain's cabin, Straz paused.

'Tom,' he muttered. 'I reckon we actually could get food to Jimmy often enough.'

Irritation filled Tom and he badly wanted to seize Straz and rattle him to pieces.

'Maybe once!' Tom whisper-yelled. 'Or even twice! But it's not like we'll be docking in Melbourne next week. And what if Jimmy dies?'

In the dull light, Tom watched Straz's frame slump.

'Want me to knock?' Tom asked. For the first time, he wondered if the captain would count this crime against them both. Straz inhaled, shook his head and trudged the last few steps, and knocked on the captain's door.

After a moment, a voice called, 'Come!'

Straz turned the handle and stepped into Gibb's cabin. Tom had been in this cabin before, on a previous voyage, scrubbing it after the captain was removed to the sickbay. It was the finest room on the ship. To the left, a good-sized bed was fixed against the inside wall, with a wardrobe at its foot. Three wide drawers on top of each other made the base of the bed and Tom knew they held all the captain's charts. White linen sheets. Silk-covered pillows. Red woollen blankets.

Opposite, attached to the ship's frame, was a French-styled soft couch with matching footstool. At head height, brass bolts held four wall lamps, all lit now even though some daylight filtered through the portholes. Fresh white paint on the walls glowed like mother-of-pearl. The door, bed and cupboards were mahogany fitted with shiny brass hooks and handles. On the desk, a glass inkbottle rested in a leather and wood tray held in place with neat wooden pegs. The inkbottle reflected a distortion of the cabin. Behind the tray, a handful of books were packed tightly on a small, railed bookshelf. One spine said *Moby Dick*.

Straz stood next to the open cabin door, which backed against another door that led into the captain's bathroom with its own basin, bathtub and privy.

Opposite the cabin door, Gibb's desk was bolted to the hull wall. The chair was pushed aside and Gibb was standing and leaning over a chart of Africa's west coast.

He half-turned and raised his eyebrows, no doubt expecting to see his steward, and not expecting to see two apprentices. He straightened up.

'Midshipmen Pearce, and Strasenburgh.' His shirt was open at the neck, crisp and white under his beard. His sleeves were rolled to his elbows.

'Captain Gibb,' Straz said. 'I'm sorry to interrupt sir, but … I need to tell you something.' Voices of a couple of passengers hummed past the space outside the cabin. 'May I shut the door, sir?'

Gibb nodded. It was a small space and Tom took a step back until he was against the wardrobe.

'Sir,' Straz said. He hesitated and looked around at Tom. He started again. 'Sir, there's a stowaway on board. And it was me who brought him on.'

Straz must have dug up a brave-Straz from somewhere.

Although Gibb did not move, a shadow passed over his face. It appeared and vanished so fast that Tom could not find a word to describe it to himself.

Gibb took a long moment to unroll his left sleeve. He picked out a silver cufflink from a drawer in his desk and inserted it into the cuff. He did the same with his right sleeve. Perhaps his routine. Perhaps a way to give himself time to think. He stepped towards his couch where he had a clear view through a porthole, and gazed out at the dark clouds and the black surging ocean. His body flowed naturally with the pitching of the ship, as though his feet were nailed to the floor.

'Please explain,' Gibb said, turning back to Straz. He flashed a glance at Tom but looked back to Straz.

'Captain, Tom didn't know until today. He got me to come to you. The stowaway is my cousin Jimmy Collingwood. And he's in the forward hatch.'

Gibb flinched slightly. 'I ordered all the hatches battened today.' The wind howled outside and whistled through gaps in the doorframe. 'And I presume that's why you're here?'

Straz straightened. 'Yes, sir.'

Gibb lifted the charts from his desk. 'Pearce, open that second draw behind you.' He nodded at his bed then slid the charts off his desk and into a broad draw that was already half full of sea charts. He flattened them out then slid the drawer closed, latched it, pulled his chair to the desk, reached for his logbook, and sat.

Everything went into the logbook. Every injury. Every illness. Birth. Death. Every turn of weather. Every latitude and longitude. Every discipline and breach of regulations.

Gibb had his back to them now. He primed his pen.

'Start again, Strasenburgh. The stowaway's full name?'

Straz's eyes met Tom's.

'Jimmy … no,' Straz stammered. 'James Collingwood, sir.'

'Age?'

'Seventeen, I think.'

Gibb sighed. 'And what day did you bring him on?'

'When we departed, when all the relatives were on the deck.'

'And,' Gibb said, twisting in his chair to look at Straz. 'How did the Customs Officers not come across him when they inspected the ship?'

'I put him in a flour barrel. It was empty,' Straz said. 'I'd added a hole for breathing. Then that night I moved him to a gap in the forward cargo hold.'

'In the flour barrel?'

'No sir. He walked.'

'What time was that?'

'Oh,' Straz looked at Tom and half shrugged. 'About near the end of the first watch that night.'

'So, around half after eleven?'

'Yes, sir.'

Gibb wrote two or three lines more into the logbook.

'And he's been in complete darkness for nearly two weeks?'

Straz didn't answer.

'There'll be more to his story,' Gibb said, 'but I want to hear it from him.' He leaned out and pulled on a tasselled rope hanging behind the door.

Within moments there was a knock and the steward, George Clay, entered.

'Yes, sir?'

'Clay, bring me the first-mate.'

'Aye, sir,' Clay said. He flashed a curious look at the two midshipmen then closed the door with a firm click.

'I assume,' Gibb said, 'that neither of you are on watch right now?'

'No, sir,' they answered together.

Barely a minute later, boots thudded in the narrow hall and a double knock landed on the door.

'Come!'

First-Mate Mac faltered as he stepped in. His eyes stabbed a question at the two midshipmen. He stood taller than the captain, and broader across the shoulders. The captain's face and Mac's each came with their own insulation against the wind and cold – dense beards. But Mac's was salt-and-pepper grey with a light-brown lick down the right where his pipe hung whenever it was not in his jacket pocket.

'Yes sir?' he rumbled.

'Mac, take handcuffs. Strasenburgh is about to show you where he's hiding a stowaway. Bring the stowaway, and Strasenburgh, back here immediately.'

Straz jolted. 'Cuffs sir? He'd be no trouble. I could bring him here without cuffs.'

'It's necessary, Strasenburgh. What would it tell everyone if I welcomed this person with open arms? That the captain encourages stowaways?' He barely looked at the door but the order was clear. Straz followed Mac out, and Tom turned to follow them.

'Wait here, Pearce.' When the door was shut again, Gibb's eyes drilled into Tom's.

'Is it true you knew nothing about the stowaway except what you've learned today?'

'Yes, sir. Straz… Strasenburgh only told me at lunch today.'

Gibb measured him. The mood changed in the cabin and the captain's body relaxed a little. 'You have a family history at sea, Pearce?'

'My step-father was a captain, sir.'

Gibb hesitated just long enough for Tom to guess he had noted the word "was".

'What ship, Pearce?' Gibb buttoned his collar. He knotted his tie.

'The *Gothenburg*. It went down in seventy-five. Most lives were lost, including his.'

'The *Gothenburg*?' Gibb stared at a wall. 'Ah yes, off the north-east of Australia?'

'Yes, sir. The great reef.'

Gibb seesawed his jacket from a hanger in the wardrobe. He gave it a quick brush with his hand and glided his body into it.

The horizon tilted back and forth beyond the porthole and lines of rain stabbed down into the ocean. The air in the cabin went silent.

CHAPTER ELEVEN

Wednesday 13 March
Tom

From a distance, the *Loch Ard* would look like a leaf floating on the watery ocean. But she was so much more than that.

In her many layers of internal decks, she carried cargo packed so tight that, apart from a few narrow walkways, there was barely room for the obligatory rats and mice. For months, she was seen from below only by fish and whales, and from above by an occasional bird and God.

The ship cradled the lives of fifty or so beating human hearts and a few animals for butchering. The wind fuelled her and the men steered her across the earth from a tiny point in the northern hemisphere, to another in the southern. Day and night the captain measured the ship's place on the sea by taking measurements from the sky back down to his maps and noting the calculations.

Tom stood stiffly in Gibb's cabin and watched him read the coordinates he'd noted in the ship's log. Then someone knocked on the door.

'Come!' Gibb said. He stood and pushed his chair under the desk as far as he could, and now Tom saw that the added collar, tie and jacket completed Gibb's authority.

'Sir,' Mac said as he pressed a handcuffed boy before him through the door. Tom made room by backing into the corner against the furthest porthole and felt shocked at how pale the boy looked. The stranger in the room stood swaying slightly with his eyes almost entirely squinted against the light, even though the captain's cabin was dull. If the boy was seventeen as Straz had said, then he was tiny for his age. A perfect size for a jockey, and a stowaway.

'You're James Collingwood?' Gibb asked.

The boy's eyes opened a hair's breadth more. He nodded.

'I need you to speak.'

'Yes, sir,' Jimmy said with a raspy voice.

'Collingwood. I'm Captain Gibb. I need to inform you, and Strasenburgh, that what you've both done is illegal.'

Straz's face twitched. Collingwood nodded.

'Yes, sir,' they said together.

Gibb glared at Jimmy. 'I hope you understand that the *Loch Ard* is not stopping at any ports on this voyage, and I refuse to lose valuable time to sail off course and deliver you to land. Unfortunately, the days are gone when it would be acceptable to throw you overboard.'

Jimmy flickered his eyes open fully for a few seconds.

'Yes, sir.'

Gibb looked at Mac.

'Mac, if you agree, Collingwood can work his keep, and I'll hand him over to the authorities at our Melbourne office when we dock. If his behaviour on this voyage is good, then we'll send a good report with him. If it's bad, I'll recommend charges be laid against him and Strasenburgh.'

Mac nodded. 'I agree, Captain,' Mac said. 'The galley could do with another pair of hands. I'll put him to work there, and wherever else he can be useful. The forward port bunkroom has a spare bunk if that's alright sir?'

Gibb nodded. He faced Straz directly. 'Strasenburgh. Maritime laws are very strict about stowaways, and even stricter about crew who aid them. The punishment I've seen recently is a public caning, plus day and night for a week in chains at the stern, and pay reduced to half.'

Tom heard Straz gasp.

'Sir?' Tom began, but Mac shook his head at him.

'Captain,' Mac said. 'If it's alright with you, I'll give Strasenburgh extra duties for the rest of the voyage, and put him on half pay.'

The rain continued to tap on the upper deck. Then there was a howl and a thud above their heads. Gibb and Mac's eyes met. Not again.

'One minute Mac, before you go and check on who's fallen this time.' Gibb felt for his pipe in his pocket. 'I like your idea.' He glared at Straz. 'Strasenburgh, I'm going to suspend your punishment. That means it's on hold for each day. If Mac reports to me that there's been even the tiniest offence during the remainder of this voyage, I'll undo the suspension immediately and apply the full punishment, which means caning and chains. Do you understand?'

Straz answered in a gurgle. 'Yes, sir.'

'And Pearce,' Gibb said, turning to Tom. 'I'm going to put you in charge of Strasenburgh and Collingwood. You're to supervise them both and make sure they fulfil any duties that Mac gives them, all the way to Melbourne. They're your responsibility. I want a written report on my desk every evening of all the duties they're given, and how well they're done.'

'Aye, Captain.' Tom would lose much of his little free time and now wished he'd sent Straz by himself.

'Mac, release the cuffs. Strasenburgh, take your cousin to the galley to arrange him proper food and drink. Pearce, please inform the doctor to check Collingwood's health. If the doctor clears him, Collingwood's duties begin tomorrow.'

'You've been very kind, Captain,' Jimmy said.

Gibb glanced at him.

'I'd best see what's happened up on deck,' Mac said, and Gibb nodded. Mac unlocked the handcuffs and left.

'You're dismissed,' Gibb said.

'Thank you, sir,' they all said. Straz led the way and led Jimmy up the soaked companionway steps towards the galley.

Tom headed for the cuddy to find the doctor.

'Doctor's gone forward to the sickbay,' a passenger told him.

Tom pulled the cuddy door closed and made his way down the narrow steps and through the hold area to the forward sickbay but a hand grabbed his arm from behind. It was Straz, alone, carrying a lantern.

'Where's Jimmy?' Tom asked. He shook his arm from Straz's grasp.

'Eating. I shouldn't have listened to you!' Straz growled. 'Extra duties. Half pay!'

'Straz, Jimmy would have died if we'd not done it.'

'Well, it's going to be pretty hard to get through a whole voyage without doing something wrong,' Straz spat. 'Especially when someone's spying on you all the time!'

'That's up to you!' Tom said. 'I'm not going to run to Gibb or Mac all the time. You're the only one to blame for what's happened, and things would've ended badly if I'd done nothing.'

Straz's shoulders lowered. His face lost some of its tightness.

'It wasn't supposed to go like this!'

'Don't forget what's happened to me,' Tom said. 'I've ended up with a heap more work every single day to Melbourne.'

CHAPTER TWELVE

The same day
Eva

The singing had surprised Eva. She'd known there'd be wind and waves, and that the ocean would serve up fish, and that they'd see whales and dolphins, and that the horizon would be a far-away band around them. But it never occurred to her that sailors would sing while they hauled on lines to hoist sails or to turn the yards. When teams were called to work the sails for a tack, one man would start a booming song and they'd all join in and match their hauling to the rhythm.

But, that day, outside, the wind howled through the lines and masts like a band of mourners and drove the ship at seven or eight knots. While the weather stormed about the *Loch Ard*, Eva and a handful of other passengers had taken refuge in the cuddy. The violence of the ocean had sent her mother and Mrs Stuckey to their cabins with sick-buckets tied against the bed legs. Eva had escorted Margaret and Annie to their cabin to play with their collection of miniature dolls. The boys had disappeared to their distant cave-like cabin and apparently were being taught to play poker by another passenger, Art Mitchell.

Rain pounded the planks of the cuddy roof but the crew had battened down the skylight hatch against the rain and it dulled the noise. In the cuddy, light from lamps flickered on the varnished walls. The mizzenmast ran up from its secret beginnings far below near the keel. It rose through each deck until it passed through the cuddy, then it appeared in daylight through the poop deck, and reached for the sky.

It was early afternoon and a young steward named Spicer dodged around the cuddy balancing a decanter of wine and some goblets, offering refreshments. He had no struggle at all with the rolling of the ship and managed it as if he were walking up and down paths through peaceful woods on land.

Raby and their father were in there, and some other passengers. Raby had a fashion catalogue in front of her, which she had grumbled was already out of date. Every minute or so she turned a page, perhaps hoping to see something she had not seen before.

Eva was beside her father reading for the third time since last winter Jane Austen's *Pride and Prejudice*.

The doctor was reviewing his surgeon's journal because the shipping company required him to record every medical activity he had with the crew and passengers and to pass on information to the captain for his log.

John Stuckey and Herb Godley were playing cards and had found they could keep them from skating away if they licked their fingers occasionally to stick the cards together. They had abandoned the chess board half an hour earlier and a white pawn still rattled back and forth across the floor.

Eight chairs were bolted down around the table. The rest were loose, and even looser now as the weather threw its temper at the ship. A couple of the men were discussing a riot that had flared up in Hyde Park just days before the *Loch Ard* cast off.

Stuckey looked up from his card hand and across at Patterson.

'It was annoying,' Stuckey said. 'My wife and I were in a hotel and watched that riot go past. The whole area was flooded with raging men then they marched off to Downing Street. For my poor wife's sake, I'm glad they did not return.'

Godley sighed. He nodded to the steward to top up his goblet. 'Well, if you're interested, I was actually right there in the thick of it.'

Eva looked up, slightly alarmed. She looked at Raby whose face had lit up at a subject that could cheat boredom.

'Yes,' Godley added. 'But we preferred to call it a demonstration, not a riot.'

'What on earth was it supposed to achieve?' asked Yates, a plumpish man with the look of a banker.

Dr Carmichael cleared his throat but did not look up.

Godley glared at Yates. 'We were demonstrating against the whole Russian thing and the war with Turkey.' Then he frowned at the card he'd just picked up.

A distant scream then a hollow thud on the deck above made them all jolt upright.

'Not another one!' The doctor grumbled. He snapped his journal shut and sprang to his feet. When he opened the door, cold air howled in from the companionway stairs. He slammed the door behind him.

Minutes later, someone knocked and a crewman stood there with his drenched sea coat pouring water onto the floor around him.

'Excuse me, Miss Carmichael?'

Eva and Raby both looked up but the man's eyes were on Eva. Raby huffed and flipped her catalogue back to the beginning.

Eva laid her book on her lap. 'Yes?'

'Miss, the doctor's asked for your help in the forward sickbay. I can lead you there if you like.'

Eva stood quickly. 'Of course. What's happened?'

'Skinner took a tumble from a boom. Broken wrist by the looks.'

Eva tugged her shawl high over her shoulders and followed the man out.

'If you like Miss, we can go through the 'tween decks and stay out of the weather.'

'Yes, thank you.'

The crewman unlatched a lantern from a peg in the passageway and led Eva forward then down some narrow steps. They wove along a cramped walkway between stacks of tightly lashed cargo.

'This way, Miss,' her guide said.

They pushed through into a space in a passageway near the *Loch Ard*'s bow.

'Just in here.' The crewman knocked on a door and left Eva to enter alone.

The sickbay was a cluttered space with a small bed against the wall. Her father stood facing away in the corner, preparing bandages. The injured man sat sideways on the bed, his feet on the floor. His left forearm lay cradled and distorted on a faded cushion on his lap. One side of his face was as pale as sailcloth and the other side was swollen, purple and bleeding in tiny rivulets. He was mid-twenties, and his long soaking hair was tied back with a grimy string. A couple of days' beard shaded the skin on his jaw.

Eva put her shawl aside and tied on an apron. 'Mr Skinner?' she said in greeting.

'Miss,' Skinner mumbled in a strained voice.

Eva's father spoke over his shoulder from the compact table where he was preparing plaster of Paris.

'Eva, laudanum first,' he said. 'Twenty drops. Then we'll wait a few minutes before we pull the wrist. I'll patch up his face after that.'

Skinner jerked his head and turned towards Eva. His eyes spilled panic. 'Pull? What do you mean pull?' The jerk moved his arm slightly and he blanched.

The doctor did not turn but spoke to the plaster he was preparing.

'Young man. My daughter will tell you how many bones are in your wrist and what we must do to fix them.'

Eva sat on a low stool beside the cot. Seeing people in pain affected her deeply, and she would be almost as relieved as him when she gave him the laudanum.

'Mr Skinner,' she said gently. 'Your wrist has eight bones that are like river pebbles nestled together in a perfect bundle. Your fall probably dislodged bones and you may have cracked one or two. The doctor must pull your wrist so the bones slip back into their places. Then he'll wrap them in a cast until your wrist is healed. A few weeks hopefully.'

Skinner's eyes floated loose for a moment as though he might pass out.

'But,' Eva added, indicating her father's medicine case beside her. 'The medicine will mean you'll barely feel a thing.'

She ran her finger along the lidded bottles in the case and located the laudanum. She counted out the drops onto a teaspoon and passed the spoon to him. He swallowed the laudanum and his face twisted terribly.

'Argh! I'll be damn cussed!' he blurted. 'It tastes bleedin' foul!'

The doctor whirled around just as the ship tipped to starboard. He grasped the beam above his head and scowled at Skinner.

'Mr Skinner! I'll ask you to watch your mouth when there's a woman in the room!'

'Oh.' He winced. 'Sorry, Miss. Sorry, Doc.'

Eva blushed. It was not unusual to hear bad language from men in pain, and even women sometimes. It was as though agony could bring out the worst in someone, even if they were normally the kindest and calmest person.

The laudanum worked quickly. Skinner's eyes became slits, and his head and shoulders slumped back against the wall. Eva anchored his arm while her father pulled on the hand. The clicking was more a feeling than a sound as the bones moved inside the wrist. The doctor ran his thumb around the bones, feeling the locations.

'It should be enough,' he said. He wrapped several layers of wet plaster bandages around it and within a few minutes it had begun to set.

'He'll return to us soon,' the doctor said, feeling the bones in Skinner's face. 'I don't think anything is broken here, just deeply bruised. Won't need stitches. I'll clean him up while the cast hardens. You can return to the cuddy if you like, Eva.'

The ocean rolled up from dark water heaving through unseen valleys far below. When Eva stepped out of the sickbay, the rain still played loudly on the deck above so she found the path back along the same winding and dry route she had come with the crewman. She stumbled along the passageway, in the dark this time, and eventually found the cuddy.

Eva hesitated before she turned the handle. For the first time since the voyage had begun, she felt useful.

'I've just had a very tiny adventure,' she whispered to herself.

CHAPTER THIRTEEN

Friday 29 March
63 days to Melbourne
Eva

The doctor was below checking on Mrs Stuckey who'd developed an illness. He had required Eva's mother to attend as well. On a protected corner of the deck, Eva and Raby sat on rubber cushions wedged between a hatch and some steps. Margaret and Annie were snuggled in with them, taking turns with their readers. Annie who was barely six could read almost as well Margaret who was ten.

The Carmichaels were one-third of the way to Melbourne, and they were all changing. Thomas had separated himself from the family. A few soft whiskers had begun to darken his chin and top lip and he refused to let his mother cut his hair that already hung over his ears and neck. Eva thought he was almost wild, and their father only ever grunted disapproval when he passed him. Evory was onto his fourth and last book and he'd already asked Eva if *Pride and Prejudice* might be worth him reading.

Even though the sea was rolling, the air was fresh and salty and there had been a few warmer days over the past week as the ship crept towards the equator.

Near the foredeck, some of the male passengers were tucked in smoking their pipes and telling stories. Rolleston, Patterson, Pitt and Godley. And Thomas Carmichael too, although he had not dared pick up a pipe, yet.

Eva leaned over Annie's shoulder to correct a word. She turned and saw Raby's gaze locked unblinkingly on something. She traced the gaze to Art Mitchell who was leaning against a mast half-listening to the conversations, half-staring out to sea. For a moment, he looked at Raby. Eva froze. Inside, she groaned.

A few months before they'd left Ireland, a young man had declared his love to Raby, but when the doctor discovered Raby's "love" he told her that he had made his decision to relocate the family just in time. Raby had wailed that she would be leaving "a piece of her heart" behind.

'You will not marry a butcher's son!' their father had said. They were on opposite sides of their dining room, standing after supper. 'A butcher cannot marry the daughter of a doctor, especially not the eldest daughter. You must get over this infatuation. If I see you together at all, I will approach his father.'

The emigration plans were falling into place and the family had soon packed up and was sailing away from the problem.

Eva dropped in a word that Annie was guessing, then raised her eyes towards the men. Art Mitchell was probably twenty-five or so. And he was perfect heart material for Raby. Young. Handsome. Mischievous.

When the reading was over and the younger girls had run off to their cabin and toys, Eva turned to Raby who was half-heartedly crocheting a hair-tie of red cotton.

'Raby,' she said. 'Be careful please.'

Raby's face questioned, then understood, then denied. 'Why?'

'You know I'm talking of Mr Mitchell. Father might lock you in our cabin for the rest of the voyage if he even gets a hint of your glances at that man today.'

Raby unhooked her thread. 'What do you mean?' she said. Her voice snapped as though it was a sail.

'Raby! You know.'

Raby huffed. Her chin crevassed. She inhaled deeply.

'Father does not care about my feelings, only his reputation.'

'Keep your voice down,' Eva muttered. 'Are you telling me you truly are drawn to Mr Mitchell?'

'I don't know.' Raby's eyes glistened. 'He seems a good man. And fair. And he likes to have fun. I know he's not from the stock Father would want … but stock's not everything.'

Eva's eyes rolled up and she paused to watch two crewmen skitter up the foremast.

'Raby!' her voice lowered to a hiss. 'Mr Mitchell's fathers and brothers are dairymen. I heard him telling Evory and Thomas yesterday. Mr Mitchell could not possibly support you in the way you need.'

'They may be dairymen! But Art is educated and has great dreams for the future. That shows he's progressive and that's good enough for me.'

'Art? Are you using Christian names already?'

Raby said nothing.

'Please take care Raby! Don't do anything reckless or I'll faint from fear of watching you all the time. We have two months before Melbourne.' Eva paused. 'If something goes wrong and Father finds out … well, I can't bear to think about it.'

Their mother's voice came from the railing near the companionway. 'If Father finds out what?'

'Oh, Mother! It's nothing,' Raby said quickly. She looked daggers at Eva. 'Just a little prank we're thinking of.'

Eva turned the conversation. 'Is Mrs Stuckey feeling better, Mother?'

Her mother sighed and sat down sideways onto one of the cushions then answered in a hushed voice.

'Mrs Stuckey has miscarried.'

'Oh,' Eva said. 'I didn't know she was expecting a child.'

'She didn't know herself until two weeks ago. She thought she was just seasick.'

'That's so sad,' Raby said. It was a rare moment for Raby to be sympathetic, but she did love tiny children.

'It is sad. She's weak but she should recover in a few days. Your father has sedated her for now and Mr Stuckey is sitting with her in the aft sickbay. We'll move her to their cabin tonight if she can eat some supper and keep it down. And we'll have to watch her for a fever.'

Eva stood and reached for her mother's hand.

'Mother, I think you need a nice cup of tea. Come Raby. We'll go and ask the steward to brew a pot for us all.'

Raby did not move. 'I'll just sit here and crochet another inch or two, then come down,' she said.

As Eva turned towards the companionway, she glared at Raby. And Raby scowled back.

Ten minutes later, and Raby still had not appeared in the cuddy. The steward poured tea for them. From the pantry, he brought out a tray covered with a white linen cloth. It bore scones and little bowls of strawberry jam and butter.

'Oh, I do prefer mine with cream,' Eva's mother said.

'I'm sorry Mrs Carmichael. This far from land we cannot have cream without a cow on board.'

'Oh, of course.' She looked at Eva. 'Raby should be here by now.'

'I'll go and see if she's in the privy, Mother,' Eva offered.

Her mother nodded. The demands of helping her husband and supporting Mrs Stuckey seemed to have worn her out.

'Check on Margaret and Annie on the way. They're sure to want some of these lovely scones.'

Eva fetched the girls first, to distract her mother. A sick feeling grew in her belly. If William had been with them, he would have kept Raby in line.

Eva grabbed the railings and stepped up to the main deck. Raby was not where she had left her. And Art Mitchell was not on the deck either.

'Are you looking for someone, Miss Eva?' It was Mac in his black linen trousers and faded dark-blue jacket all buttoned in silver.

Sails. Ropes. Hatches. Masts. They all blurred in her vision and she didn't know what to say.

'Miss? Are you right? Shall I fetch your father?'

'I'm so sorry, Mr McLauchlan. I'm quite well. It's the ocean. It made me dizzy for a moment.' Her heart pounded with frustration inside her chest. Not just the ocean.

'Just breathe deeply Miss and look at the waves. They're quite calming once you've watched them for a while.'

Then Eva spotted Raby forward near the hencoop talking with Mr Stuckey who must have come up while his wife was resting.

'Thank you. I feel better already.'

She raised a hand to Raby who saw her and made her way carefully aft. Her green sewing bag dangled from her wrist and her eyes were alight. Despite the movement of the ship, her steps were light and cheery.

'It's such a lovely day,' she said, looking across the water.

'Raby, Mother's asking where you've got to. The tea is ready.'

'Well, I did talk for a minute or two with Art. But that's all. Nothing more than a conversation about the weather.'

The light dropped from her eyes. 'Then Mr Stuckey came on deck and I asked after poor Francis. She's sleeping now.'

The ship rolled to port and the girls gripped to the companionway railing.

'I'll go for tea,' Raby said. She paused. 'But Eva, you're not my superior! I won't take to you ordering me about.' Then she swished around and stomped down the steps.

Above Eva's head, each sail on each mast was full of air. The wind blew across her face.

'Blow harder,' she said to the wind. 'We need to get there fast.'

CHAPTER FOURTEEN

'What's it this time?' Straz baited. 'Food, or ale?'

'Definitely food,' Tom said. 'I'll be extra hungry after I've beaten you.'

'Doubt it,' Straz said. He shook out his arms.

Even at dawn, the varnished wood of the bunkroom was hot against Tom's back, and the deck warmed the soles of his bare feet. This was the starting point for their races, and the heat of the equator was not going to stop them.

One morning, a week after the turmoil of finding Jimmy Collingwood, Straz had woken up, stared at the ceiling of the bunkroom for a while, then apologised to Tom for everything. Since then, despite coming from different ends of the earth, they became like brothers. They told one another stories of their childhood, talked about their dreads and dreams, and almost daily raced each other up one mast or another.

'You ready?' Tom asked. Without listening for an answer, he yelled, 'Go!'

He ran to the left and Straz to the right. They leapt onto opposite shrouds of the main mast and clambered hand over hand up the rope ladder. On the deck, a few men smoking their first pipe for the day shaded their eyes and watched.

Elated, Tom reached the top first and whacked his hand on the wooden lookout just a bare second before Straz.

Straz's chest was heaving. He grimaced. 'So, you want … my bread … or my potato?'

'How about half of each?'

'Sounds fair, but don't get used to it … Next time, it'll be your ale.'

They climbed down. Straz went to the bunkroom. Tom leaned at the rail and watched the sweep of sky brighten. The drift of change from night to day could lift the dullest soul voyaging across the oceans. And drifting was what they were doing now, because, on this dawn, the *Loch Ard* travelling to Melbourne was entirely stationary.

In the middle of nowhere. Going nowhere.

The watch crew were vaguely at their stations. Billy Johnson, the cook's-mate, was at the wheel – a joke of Mac's. Billy hated being on the poop deck. Any deck. His favourite places were dark places, like his bunkroom, the galley, or when he was running errands below deck in the half-light. But the wind had not blown for two days so Mac had decided to make Billy steer the ship – particularly because they were not going anywhere.

Billy sat gloomily beside the wheel. His eyes were closed and his head leaned against the timbers of the wheelhouse.

The air was humid and smelled of hot wood and tar, and the sun promised more for later. It was the sort of heat that brought the worst out of the best people.

Several sails dangled limply above, with the vague hope that a puff of wind would enlarge them slightly. On Thursday, when their speed had dropped below three knots, the crew had rigged a few small sails horizontally six feet above the decks to shade the humans and animals on board. Only a few hours later, the *Loch Ard* had slowed to yards then feet, then stopped.

Tom felt uneasy. He listened to the sound of the ship becalmed. From just above the waterline came the drip of seawater falling off the hull and into the ocean as she tilted almost invisibly, inch by inch, left then right, slightly up, slightly down on the tiny swell over the deep black-green where the North and South Atlantic Oceans merged. He could hear too the irritating creaks of planks and masts and yards and booms.

The earth spun minute by minute towards the sun – a great orb that sneaked its crest up through the eastern horizon. The light turned parts of the masts and sails to gold. Then the rooster crowed, and his voice carried across the sea, as though the whole world should hear him. Tom imagined the sound jolted the last of the passengers and crew from anxious sleep and sweat-soaked clothes.

Captain Gibb trod up the companionway steps. He wore no jacket. His sleeves were rolled perfectly to neat bands above his elbows. He walked a slow, full lap of the ship. He greeted each person with a silent nod. None of the crew pretended to work.

Horrible stories hung in the back of minds that rarely reached their lips. Stories of ships found floating on an ocean and whose only answer to 'Ahoy!' was the crackling of human bones rolling about the decks. Or stories of mutiny by desperate men, trimming the number of people on board until the remaining food and water stood a chance of lasting longer than the lack of wind.

Fear and boredom were their enemies. And soon Mac would make sure the crew would be hard at it again with scrubbing and tarring and endless tasks.

Even the ship seemed irritated. Her bow pointed stubbornly south rather than east and refused to turn. Without wind, she could wallow there for days, or weeks.

On the far west horizon, a long line of cloud – the fading edge of a too-distant storm – lingered and would probably tease them for a while then disappear again. The earth nudged another click on its axis. The sun began to drape its molten heat.

Gradually, more passengers dragged themselves up the steps to look about. They stared sadly at the mirror sea.

Water and food were rationed now and it taxed moods further.

Giles put coal into the galley fire and got it burning to bake bread, and the humans groaned. Smoke from the stovepipe lingered over the deck, punishing them all.

Late morning, Tom was still barefoot with rolled-up sleeves and trousers. He was halfway to the top of the foremast on the starboard side painting some of the shroud lines. Sweat ran from under his hat, through his hair, down the sides of his face then soaked into his collar. Below him six men scrubbed the deck boards with sand and seawater. Straz, Jimmy and some others were washing the upturned hulls of the two lifeboats lashed onto skids on the bunkroom. Here and there about the deck, men polished each and every brass fitting on the ship's wheel, the bell, the binnacle, and even the door hinges and latches.

The passengers did what they could to cope. Most of the women had gone below so they could remove their outer layers of clothing and rest on their beds. Men sat in shirt sleeves under the shade fanning themselves with newspapers.

Then the peace broke. Small shoes tapped fast on the companionway steps. The two youngest Carmichael girls clattered up from below, giggling. They hit the deck full of energy, and tore off, one after the other, zig-zagging around the hatches and up the steps onto the fo'c'sle, squealing and tagging each other, then rushing away. Their noise jarred the air as Tom watched them. Flashes of white dresses appeared and disappeared between the horizontal sails. The girls seemed unaffected by the heat and were up to their usual unsupervised games of running amok.

Then a man above Tom yelled, 'Dolphins. Starboard bow!'

Most eyes shifted lazily towards the water. Just yards away, a pod of seven or eight dolphins rose like huge, black chain-links through the shiny surface. Water skated off their skin and merged into the sea.

Then the air on the ship cracked with a guttural scream and Tom's skin prickled.

A crewman yelled, 'She's gone over!' Alarmed eyes snapped towards the bow where little Annie stood alone and motionless on the fo'c'sle.

Directly out from Tom a cloud of bubbles was dissolving into the sea.

Barely aware, he hurled his tar bucket away into the ocean, squatted deeply and leapt far out to dive clear of the railing below. His hat flew off. His hands then body targeted the green-white fizz of Margaret's dress as it faded into the hungry, deep darkness that measured many miles to the sea floor. He closed his eyes and his arms sliced through the surface.

For an instant, he was eleven again. It was a hot January day and he had dived into the Yarra two hundred yards from the brickworks. The water cooled his flesh. That part of the river was deep and he felt the water behind him pulse as his school friend dived in too.

He opened his eyes. Here, in the ocean, the water was not the muddy brown like under the jetty on the Yarra. It was the profound green of the Atlantic.

Fear mixed with hope as he gained on the girl. His arms pulled hard arcs, hauling him deeper. His legs kicked fast, propelling him and he was glad he'd been barefoot all day. He couldn't go much further before he would have to return to breathe. His angle was vertical. Margaret's was horizontal.

He reached her and snapped his arm around her waist. And the hardest part became changing their momentum. To stop. To fight up instead of down. His lungs were screaming to breathe. His legs scissored hard and the shock of the chill water threatened to cramp his muscles.

It took almost too many of the longest seconds of his life to fight to the surface and he breached it to the roar of his own gasp for air and then to splashing and action. The girl was limp and silent against him. Her head flopped heavily on his shoulder. Her hair floated across his face and around his throat.

Three men were in the water. They were yelling at him and he could not immediately translate. Men were calling from the fo'c'sle. Someone tossed a life-ring and it landed with a large splash beside Tom. He and the other men forced it over Margaret's sagging head and arms while a row of desperate faces watched from the rail. Men on board pulled on the rope attached to it and began to haul her aboard.

A Jacob's ladder clattered over the rail and knocked against the hull.

Tom climbed the ladder. Hands reached and hauled him on board. He sank onto the deck against the hull, breathing deeply. Trembling.

Not far away, they had Margaret on her belly beside the windlass. Her unseeing face pointed at Tom and turned his insides cold. Blood leaked from a small welt on her forehead, perhaps from the way she had landed on the water.

Annie was sat nearby like a stone, and Thomas and Evory hovered behind their father who was on his knees beside Margaret using cupped hands to strike her back over and over again.

'Come on, girl!' he growled. 'Come on!'

He shoved his arms under her abdomen and jerked her whole body up, then all but dropped her with unexpected violence before slapping at her back again.

The ship was mute, and the hush of the ocean amplified how far the *Loch Ard* languished from the rest of the world. The only noise came from the doctor's frantic hands.

Then bare footsteps on wood.

Mrs Carmichael rushed towards them, her feet pattering on the timber. Her hair was undone and flowed behind her. She wore a lightweight, floral robe over her petticoat. She fell on her knees beside them.

'Margaret. My darling! Wake up! Please,' she begged. 'Wake up.'

The captain moved in close but, like every other soul on board was helpless except to mouth a silent prayer.

Then, almost impossibly a hiccup popped from Margaret's throat. A little cough. Then a bigger one. Water bubbled around her lips.

Tom stood up, unsteady.

'Thank God,' her father said. He rubbed vigorously at her back and slapped at it until the girl vomited seawater, then breakfast, into a pool around her face that soaked into her mother's robe.

The older sisters arrived and rushed to their mother.

And then something happened to the air.

At first, Tom thought he was just feeling goose bumps from the almost catastrophe. But the goose bumps stayed. Then the other men who had jumped into the water, who were now standing nearby, showed signs that they had noticed the change as well. A slight chill on one edge of their wet bodies. One by one they glanced at each other. A little slap of air cooled the right of Tom's soaked body. A puff of a breeze.

Aloft, a sail flapped. Each crewman and some passengers turned their faces up. They stared at the sails padding in and out. Tiny puffs of air. The ship tilted a few inches down at port and a few people staggered and grasped at railings or ropes.

'Wind!' Mac yelled. He raced back along the ship, up the poop deck steps and to the wheel. Billy had stayed there, as he should have, and Mac ripped his hand away and spun the wheel to turn the ship east. All the watch crew ran to their locations on the deck or up the shrouds.

Mac bellowed, 'Ready about. Mainsail haul.'

Gibb put his hand on the doctor's shoulder and said something then strode aft towards the poop deck. Above, the sails popped and, apart from a minute earlier when the girl had begun to breathe, it was the best sound anyone had heard for days.

Tom stood and tried to convince his shaking legs to walk.

Baxter came up to him. 'Not you Pearce. We'll cover your watch.'

'I think I'll be alright,' Tom said.

'No. Sit it out.'

Tom found somewhere to sit. Within a minute the ship began to creep along as though it had never been becalmed and over the next few minutes the speed crept from one knot to three.

Dr Carmichael hoisted his daughter into his arms and carried her aft towards the companionway and their cabin.

Tom stared at the ocean where the water was far deeper than their longest lead-line could measure. If the girl had fallen just a few minutes later, in the minutes after the wind had come rather than in those before, she would soon be the subject of a memorial at sea.

At noon, he joined the queue for the midday meal.

An hour later, the bell rang to gather everyone. There were no Carmichaels in the gathering.

Mac stood at the poop. 'We have good news. If the wind stays up, we'll pass the equator in the next couple of hours.' He paused. 'So, this evening, even though we'll have barely a quarter moon, we'll have a moonlit party on deck.' Folk cheered. 'A bonus ration of ale or spirits for the crew.' A louder cheer, mostly from up the masts. 'And for our adult passengers, bonus wine and brandy.' A few men on deck clapped their hands. 'And,' Mac added, 'dessert for everyone!'

Giles the cook backed away and stomped off to the galley. There was the sound of a pan striking the stove and Giles yelling at Jimmy.

Later that afternoon, when it was too hot to nap in the deckhouse, Tom was laid out resting under a sail shade near the fo'c'sle. He was awake with his eyes closed.

'Excuse me, Tom.'

Tom opened his eyes. Evory Carmichael was crouched in front of him and Tom sat up. The boy was lankier than when he'd come on board. Tanned too.

'Evory,' Tom said. 'Is something wrong with your sister?'

'No. Not at all.' He held a book on his thigh. 'My father asked me to find you, to thank you for rescuing Margaret. He'll probably come and see you sometime soon, anyway, but he didn't want you to think he'd forgotten.'

'Oh,' Tom said. 'It was just …'

'Father said you might be all "it's just part of the job" but he's asked me to thank you on behalf of our family. He's shocked that one of us nearly drowned out here. So, anyway,' and he looked a little sheepish, 'I'd like to give you this.' He held out the book. 'I think you'll enjoy it.'

Tom took it and the feel of the cover reminded him of his sailing book in his sea chest. He turned it around and read its spine. *Five Weeks in a Balloon* by Jules Verne.

'Thank you, Evory. I hope your sister is alright.'

'She is. I think Father's more worried about Mother now. She's gone all nervous and jittery.'

'Understandable.' Tom felt a little nervous and jittery himself.

'Anyway, thanks,' Evory said, and he left.

So the *Loch Ard* skated slowly south-east, sailing into its first hundred miles of the southern hemisphere. Supper blended into the night party and the minimal moon trickled the ocean with a magical stream of gold scattered with tiny diamonds and splinters of silver.

Around nine o'clock, someone rang the bell. Gibb stood at the front of the poop and waited. Lanterns illuminated yellow faces that were turned towards him. He beckoned at Tom.

'Midshipman Pearce,' he said when Tom, embarrassed, reached the top of the steps. Gibb looked over the deck and then round at those behind him. He was in his full uniform despite the hot night. 'Tom, your swift action saved a young life today and I'll be recommending you for a medal when we reach Melbourne. I've logged the event, but I've also written a detailed letter to be forwarded to the Merchant Navy when we land, to go on your permanent record. But for now, I'm recognising to everyone on board your ability on and in the water, and your bravery.'

Atkinson, who was on a boom above Tom, led out "Three Cheers".

As soon as he could, Tom melted back to the queue that had formed for dessert that turned out to be a choice of treacle pudding served with thick, sweet custard, suet pudding dobbed with melted butter and a sprinkle of sugar, or rice pudding with currants and raisins, browned on top to a crisp. The food seemed to have improved even more since the stowaway had been allocated to the galley.

After the party, the passengers played charades. Far forward, most of the men sang away their liquor ration then, much later, staggered back to their bunks. And the *Loch Ard* sliced at a gentle speed quietly towards Melbourne.

CHAPTER FIFTEEN

Monday 29 April
32 days to Melbourne
Eva

Two months had passed since the day Eva had felt the *Loch Ard* creep away from the pier at Gravesend. Now on this warm mid-morning she sat on a cushion on the foredeck reading *Twenty Thousand Leagues Under the Sea* that Evory had loaned her. He'd filled almost all the margins with pencilled notes and Eva had to concentrate hard to try to ignore them. She breathed in the air that smelled of salt, not of the grass and meadows she missed so much. The breeze was stronger at the front of the ship, but from her spot there she could view the ocean the best.

The sounds of the Loch Ard had become a familiar part of her life – the ship's bell clanging its codes to the crew, the orders bellowing from the wheel, the singing sailors, and the almost never-ending adjusting of ropes and sails.

A whoop filled the air above her. Eva shielded her eyes and squinted up. She spotted the sailor – Tom Pearce – who had rescued Margaret. He'd not shown a moment of pride about it and it was though nothing unusual had happened at all.

He was up high with another one – Shulenburgh? – no, Strasenburgh. They were climbing fast on separate masts, occasionally eyeing each other, and scooting past grumbling men who were trying to work. It occurred to Eva that she'd seen these two do this before, but had always thought they were working and now she realised they were racing.

It looked like Strasenburgh had won, but then they began to descend even faster than when they went up, so the race seemed to be to the top then back to the deck again. And Pearce had the advantage. He was slightly more sure-footed, and seemed to know where to put his hands and feet without having to look at them. He landed laughing on the deck a hair sooner than Strasenburgh and a few male passengers applauded them before swinging back to their conversations.

Eva smiled to herself and returned to her reading.

'Interesting book?' asked a voice close to her ear.

She had subconsciously been toying with the thought of a cup of tea in the cuddy, but she startled and slammed the book shut. Beyond the man, a few passengers looked like they were also thinking of a pot of tea in the cuddy and were packing up and moving that way.

'Oh, Mr Jones!'

'Good morning, Miss Eva.' Jones knuckled a swathe of moist hair up his brow then reached out to help Eva to her feet.

He stood for a moment looking past her at the sea. He always looked a little hunched, and stayed as close to the midline of the ship as he could. His eyes were dark and sunken, as though he hardly ever slept.

'Have I told you how much I hate being at sea?' Jones went on.

'I don't believe so, Mr Jones.'

'I keep having a terrible nightmare that I won't make it to Melbourne. That none of us will.'

The weather was fine. A constant breeze edged them south. The ocean swelled kindly. If it were stormy, any of the passengers might say how nervous they were. He offered his hand again and helped Eva down the foredeck steps to the main deck, then immediately centred himself on the ship and leaned his back to a deckhouse wall.

Eva gripped the book at her side.

'Now, Mr Jones,' she said. 'Don't think too much of fear but tell me why you're emigrating so far away to Australia?'

For a moment, Jones's mind seemed to go back to England. Back to land and to normal. And for a moment his skin flushed pink instead of its constant pale.

'Well,' he said. 'You see, my father works on the docks near Greenwich. About eight years ago he placed me in an apprenticeship as a clerk to one of the merchants there. Once I graduated, the merchant decided to add me to his office in Melbourne. When I realised I'd have to be at sea for so long – and you can see how much I hate sailing – I invested most of my savings into acquiring a first-class cabin, where I feel a little safer.'

Tiny beads of sweat glistened on his cheek bones.

'But I just can't shake the thought that we won't make it there.'

'Mr Jones?' Captain Gibb said, stepping along from the side of the deckhouse. Jones straightened up.

Gibb smiled at Eva.

'Miss Eva. I hope you've had a nice morning,' he said. He glanced at the cushion in the bow.

'I have, Captain Gibb. A perfect morning for reading.' Then, beyond the captain's shoulders, Eva watched Raby cross the deck and turn sharply down the steps that led to the cargo hold. Raby was not wearing her usual day outfit but one of her favourite dresses – dark blue with green silk trim on the cuffs and neck.

'And Mr Jones,' Gibb said, with an edge of warning. 'I hope you're staying cheerful.' His mouth was smiling at Jones but his eyes were annoyed. It seemed he was always watching. Always aware.

'Trying to, Captain.'

Eva did not hear what the men said next. She tilted her head slightly to see past the deckhouse and her belly knotted when Art Mitchell turned down the same companionway Raby had taken. Pressure grew in Eva's skull.

'Excuse me, Captain,' she said. She forced a smile. 'I'll leave you and Mr Jones to talk. Happy thoughts Mr Jones.'

She heard Gibb say, 'Reginald, I've asked you to keep your concerns …' but another relay of orders thundered from the poop deck and the conversation was lost.

Eva's eyes took several seconds to adjust to the darkness as she descended the steps to the cargo deck.

Boots thrummed inches above her head, and voices drummed across the companionway behind her. If Raby and Mitchell were meeting in private … Eva could barely think of the consequences. She moved quietly, wanting to challenge them before their father discovered the two. She felt sick, and frustrated.

The thought of having to confront her sister, and probably Mitchell too, made her heart pound against her ribs like a hundred horses.

Above her head, someone jumped onto the deck and she almost fainted. She inhaled and steadied herself against a stack of barrels.

Behind her, the passageway led aft. In front of her, cargo choked the hold. Dozens of tea chests, more barrels, and boxes of every size were packed tight and divided through the middle by the slim passageway leading forward – the same path she took weeks ago in the storm to help bandage Skinner.

A step at a time she began to move forward. At first, she heard nothing then, after another dozen steps, she heard pieces of sentences. The sounds became whispered words then nothing.

A strange numbness wandered through Eva's belly. Her fingers tingled. She held Evory's book to her chest. So selfish of Raby. Had apathy overtaken her? Fury unfolded and Eva hoped her sister would be grateful that it was not their father plunging into this awkward meeting.

Then, without warning, her own shadow grew in front of her.

A light. From behind. She turned at the sound of a tread of shoes and the book slipped from her hand. Light spilled towards her from a lantern.

'Eva!'

'Oh. Father. How …?'

'Annie cannot help herself chattering about all the things she sees happening on this ship.' He spoke in full voice. 'I nearly ignored her again. Yet, am I correct that your older sister is somewhere down here, in the company of a man?'

The lantern swayed from an iron ring grasped in his left hand, and his right fist gripped the cane he'd hardly touched since they'd left Gravesend.

'Where is Raby?' His lips were tight. His eyes smouldered. His face was concrete and words were staccato through his teeth.

'Your sister. Where is she?'

'Father! Raby. I …' Panic swamped Eva. And their voices must surely have bounded forward to the other pair. She imagined a silent panic, then she realised that, for Raby and Art to have gone to these lengths to hide themselves, they had most likely also trapped themselves amongst the cargo.

'Go to your mother!' Her father began to press past her, then he stopped so close to her that the oil flame heated Eva's right cheek. She could smell the bergamot water he slapped around his neck multiple times a day, and she could see his chest rise and fall fast, as though he had been running, but more likely because of the anger pounding through him.

'On second thought,' he said, 'stay! You'll learn a lesson I prefer not to give to you also. Why on earth did the good Lord think I'd have the energy to raise four daughters?'

He clumped forward, became a silhouette then disappeared beyond a corner of tea chests. Eva scrabbled her hands on the floor and found the book she'd dropped.

She heard a squeal.

'Oh, Father!' Raby said.

'Mr Mitchell.' Eva barely recognised her father's voice. It was primal. Guttural.

Then a weak answer from Art Mitchell. 'Dr Carmichael! I …'

'Mr Mitchell! How dare you attempt this sabotage of my daughter's honour!'

'Sir! I love …'

A stifled squeal that could have been either man.

Raby dared to interrupt. 'But, Father!'

'Do not say "But Father" to me! I know your mother has communicated appropriate behaviour to you, so I can only assume Mr Mitchell has convinced you to behave in a manner entirely unworthy of a Carmichael.'

A sound like a gunshot echoed along the passageway, and absolute silence followed it. Eva wondered if the cane had survived whatever object it had struck.

Her father's voice erupted one word at a time. 'Mr Mitchell, do I need to say more?'

'May I answer, sir, for Ra … for Miss Carmichael and myself?'

'For the sake of me behaving like a gentleman, you may speak one sentence. And it best be short.'

'Dr Carmichael, your daughter and I have great affection for one another, but we hid it because we expected opposition due to my family's position; and I have not damaged her honour at all, except for a single kiss.'

Eva leaned one ear into the shadows. Her heart pounded louder than the sea. Would Raby say more or had she decided that silence was safer?

'You being down here in the dark with any woman, Mr Mitchell, is enough to damage her honour,' and their father's tone was like iron. 'You were correct about opposition.' There was an exhausting pause. 'Raby. This ends here. When we land in Australia, your future will take you in a separate direction to Mr Mitchell's. Then you will find, with our help, someone from a far better class.'

'But Father?' she sobbed.

'Mr Mitchell, this is a small ship but for the remainder of this voyage you are to not to be anywhere near my daughter, unless there is a person standing between you and her.'

Someone sputtered.

'Do you understand?'

There were shuffling sounds.

'I do, Doctor, but my sentiments will spend the rest of this voyage in protest.'

'Art,' Raby said. 'You'd better go.'

Mitchell trod towards the stern, and towards Eva. The lantern followed behind him. It illuminated Eva's face and Art Mitchell groaned as he met her.

'Miss Eva,' he said in whispered greeting. She bobbed her head in slight acknowledgement. His feet clumped up the distant steps and merged with others on the deck.

Their class.

Until now social class meant respect about town, and the first options for good schools, even for the Carmichael girls, except poor Annie with her fits who would probably only ever learn at home.

Perhaps, though, social class could be an enemy when some form of true love struck unexpectedly.

Raby and their father stepped towards her. When Raby saw Eva, the look on her face swung from shock to suspicion and Eva knew it was going to take a long explanation to convince Raby of her rescue attempt.

CHAPTER SIXTEEN

Monday 13 May
18 days from Melbourne
Tom

Tom zig-zagged along the deck and headed for his bunkroom. The day before, after several days of blue sky and moderate wind, heavy grey clouds had loomed in from the west. The rain had started and had not stopped and the ship had begun to lurch like a drunk, often being so deep in the hollows of waves that the entire horizon was lost.

Tom bounced side to side from the mast to the galley to a rail and finally grasped the door knob, snatched at the door frame, and hurled himself over the water board at the bottom and into his bunkroom. The door slammed itself behind him.

Chaos reigned. More than the usual squalor. He was alone, soaked. Then horrified. At boot level, a hook that was supposed to fasten a rope to keep the sailors' sea chests in place under the lower bunks had ripped from the bunk leg. The broken rope hung in two tangles and the sea chests were tumbling back and forth across the space of the floor at the mercy of the tilt and plunge of the ship. Two chests had spilled out entirely. One was Tom's. The contents were littered across the floor and each lurch of the *Loch Ard* was destroying further the things the sea chests were supposed to keep safe.

Each sailor's sea chest held his world. His history. His present. His tomorrow. For most of the year, the sea chest was the sailor's life. Childhood. Wife. Family. Personal papers. Spare clothes.

The mess on the floor sickened Tom. His letters were soiled and crushed. They were from his mother including the last one she'd sent him from San Francisco that he'd received in Gravesend just a few days before they'd cast off. And there was his book on the *Theory and Practice of Seamanship*, open and skating about facedown and creasing and mashing the pages. There was the leather diary that had belonged to his father, Richard Millett, buckled closed. And his step-father's silver watch, wrapped in a piece of felt tied with brown string. Both men were dead and these things were Tom's treasures.

To hold his father's diary in his hands was to be tugged in a blink back to a time when things were happy. To a place of innocence and childhood when his father went to work each morning and returned home to his wife and children each evening. When supper of stew, and scone bread, and fresh peas from the garden, was eaten near the theatre of kookaburras laughing and treecreepers chortling in the red-box and ironbark branches beyond the garden in rural Victoria.

And the silver watch of his step-father reminded him of a man who rescued Tom's family from destitution.

Also on the floor was Tom's own diary that he wrote in at random times plus a copy of his apprenticeship agreement folded into a yellowing envelope, a few spare items of clothing, a small sewing kit, and a small leather-covered Gospel of Matthew. Normally his foul-weather clothes would be there too – the oilskin coat and sou-wester hat – but he was wearing them.

All these thoughts filled Tom's mind in the moment or two after he had leapt through the doorway.

The ship tilted on the side of a wave and hurled the two chests and their scattered contents to port and under George's bunk. Tom crashed against the door, regained his balance, ripped off his hat and coat and tossed them onto a hook. He scooped out everything he could from under the beds, sorted his items back into his chest to tidy later, and closed the lid. His name – T. PEARCE – was stencilled in black on the faded green lid. The remaining items went into the other sea chest, which belonged to Dick Hunt. A few tools, clothing, a journal, and one tiny, blue-stitched sheepskin shoe that must have belonged to an infant. Tom rested it briefly in his palm and wondered where the other shoe was. He placed it on Hunt's other belongings in the chest and latched the lid closed.

He'd have to explain and he hoped Hunt would understand that Tom's sighting of these precious items was an accident.

CHAPTER SEVENTEEN

A quilt of clouds hung above the lonely ship. Salty haze shrouded the view. But Tom's keen eyes stared at the grey water three hundred yards away and saw the movement again. A dark glistening mass broke through the surface, then another.

They had seen whales a few times on the voyage and it always excited the passengers, and probably still would now on the last day before the southern rim of Australia would grow on the horizon. As long as the wind held, tomorrow they'd be sailing into Hobsons Bay.

Below, some passengers had hung clothes on makeshift lines to air them before packing. A few men sat smoking pipes and taking in their last full day at sea.

'Whales!' Tom yelled down. 'Whales! Port stern!'

Every passenger on deck rushed to port and watched the seven or eight whales head north-west, propelling their huge bodies out of the water, spouting then lunging heavily to split the ocean into mirrored waves. Soon they were dots then gone.

Tom's shift was nearly over. Seeing the whales had cheered him a little. Since he had woken that morning, he'd had an empty feeling inside and he realised it was probably because for the first time ever he was returning home to no one. Another family would be in their old house and it would be more than a year before Tom's apprenticeship would be over and he could join a ship to America to see his mother and siblings.

It was a relief to be high above the deck and above the stink of fresh paint and tar that Mac had ordered again. No surface had escaped being painted, tarred or polished in the past few days. The *Loch Ard* was like a new ship because a clean and ordered ship sailing into a harbour meant better ticket sales for the next destination. A ship that dared dock with peeling paint, blotched rust and dried salt could be bad for business. Gibb wouldn't know yet how many tickets the Glasgow General Shipping Company had sold for the next voyage, so this final clean was vital for his own reputation and the ship's.

The year before, Tom had watched as waiting journalists on the docks had leapt in front of disembarking passengers and asked for their stories about the ship and the voyage. By the next day, the passengers' tales, good and bad, had appeared in newspapers like the *Argus* and the *Herald* and then over the coming days in other smaller newspapers across the country. This annoying form of journalism put fear into every shipping company.

The bell rang below and Tom waited for the new watchman to climb the rigging for his watch.

His father had been a surveyor and, until he died, had taught Tom the rules of geometry. The skills, instead of steering Tom towards surveying, now made learning ship navigation so much easier. He looked out at the distant mist and could not imagine doing anything else in the world. His only goal was to become a captain and nothing could change that.

A lost gull screeched then circled the ship a couple of times before it flew away.

Tom rested his hands on the lookout frame and peered to the north knowing that Australia lay maybe fifty or eighty miles away.

On the poop deck, the captain and Mac were gathering the noon readings. The clouds made the sextant powerless so calculations were being taken from the compass, the wind direction, and the *Loch Ard*'s speed and bearing since their last check. From Tom's apprenticeship studies, he knew they'd get a close estimate of their location and could probably predict down to the exact hour when they'd enter the harbour. Gibb closed the book and headed down the aft companionway towards his cabin, which would be a dangerous exercise because the passengers were packing their travelling trunks and the passageways were crammed with belongings.

'Hey! Wake up.' Tom's replacement had arrived at the lookout.

Tom clambered down to the deck to discover Dr Carmichael waiting for him.

'Excuse me Tom,' the doctor said. He'd called Tom by his first name since Margaret's rescue.

'Hello, Doctor,' Tom said.

'I hear you're from Melbourne.'

'Yes, from South Yarra.'

The buttons on the doctor's jacket no longer gaped between each buttonhole as they had when they left England. Ship's food and fresh air had trimmed his shape to fit better inside his clothes.

'It's the logistics, you see,' the doctor said, 'of when we land. I have my wife, daughters and sons, so there are eight of us to travel to a hotel with all our belongings.'

'Well,' Tom said. 'Depending on what other ships are in harbour, we'll either tie up at the Sandridge or Williamstown pier,' Tom said. 'The train stops at both and would take you to the Melbourne station. Once you get there, you might need two or three cabs to go up to town. And don't worry about your belongings except what you need for that night. We'll unload the ship then your trunks will be carted to the address you supply the purser.'

The doctor kneaded his neat beard. 'Right then. That's very helpful. Thank you, Tom.' He turned to leave. 'Oh, do you know a decent hotel?'

'Sorry, sir. I don't. But the shipping office at the port, or a cab driver, will know the better places. When you get there, you can send a telegram back to the *Loch Ard* so we know where to send your luggage.'

Then Miss Eva approached with a message about an unwell passenger. The doctor nodded at her.

'Thank you, Tom,' the doctor said turning back to him, and he walked towards the sickbay.

Miss Eva lingered for a moment. 'In case I don't get another chance … Mr Pearce, I just wanted to thank you again – for everything.' Tom knew she meant Margaret. He was glad she didn't say it though.

'Thank you, Miss Eva. I hope your family settles well to life in Australia.'

'I'm sure we will.'

He headed to his bunkroom and realised that, despite the stowaway, a few storms and the becalming, this voyage had been the most uneventful he had ever been on.

CHAPTER EIGHTEEN

8 pm Friday 31 May
In the Grand Ocean south of Victoria
Eva

Haze filled the night sky. When the wind gusted, it slapped at anything in its way. But Eva stood determined near the main mast. She inhaled the cool salt air and soaked in the chill on her face.

It warmed her to hear the crew party forward in the 'tween deck. The sailors, except those on watch, were each enjoying their bonus mug of liquor. Burly, cheerful songs leaked along the ship, sung to an old concertina and interrupted with jokes and raucous laughter.

Eva had escaped to the deck for a few minutes but, after another deep breath of crisp air, she waved to the captain near the wheelhouse and went down to the cuddy where the passengers were celebrating their final night at sea. Normally the party was for first-class only, but Mrs Carmichael had refused to have her sons miss out, so then had to invite Art Mitchell to join them.

The doctor fumed. Raby glowed. And with the little girls flitting about the room too, all seventeen passengers were in a space that was most comfortable with less than a dozen.

Earlier, Dr Carmichael had sent Evory and Thomas to accompany the steward into the luggage hold to fetch the small cask of sherry he had reserved for this last evening, and even the little ones were enjoying a thimbleful diluted with water. They would sleep soundly when their mother eventually ordered them to bed.

Jones stood and offered Eva his chair and went and sat between Mitchell and Godley. His face had struggled all day between anxiety and relief.

Eva watched as astonishing food came on trays from Giles' galley, some of it the result of the recent slaughter of the last animals – so, mutton pie and roasted chicken. There were seared tuna steaks too, and onion and suet pudding, and steamed carrots, roasted potatoes and thick gravy. On the table in racks sat grinders of salt and pepper, bottles of Worcestershire Sauce, jugs of water, and bottles of the best wine from France. The dinner finished with a moist and tangy citrus cake with warm, sweet sauce poured over it, prepared by the stowaway. They ate and drank at leisure, hip-to-hip, shoulder-to-shoulder and, after the steward cleared the plates and the two children were escorted away, the men lit their pipes and the women did not send them outside.

Then the evening crumbled to very cramped charades and most had a go, dissolving into unfettered laughter, and even Eva's father had to use his kerchief to mop delighted tears from his cheeks. Raby played the tiny piano in the corner and snuck quick smiles to Art Mitchell. Dr and Mrs Carmichael, and Mr and Mrs Stuckey, somehow danced around the table, tumbling into chairs and people as the ship plunged forwards towards a new beginning for them all.

While the light glinted off the cuddy-sized chandelier fixed above the table, discussions popped up about the new life in Australia. Some were heading to the goldfields or to new jobs. Dr Carmichael said his family would settle to their new life in Sydney, but first they would lodge for a few weeks in Melbourne to spend time with their eldest son, William. He said it proudly, and Eva saw her mother smile.

Eva slipped out of the cuddy and used the passengers' privy. Mac's voice up on deck hollered an order and his voice carried down the companionway. He called for the sails to be shortened, and the curiosity was too much for Eva. She snatched her jacket from her cabin and climbed the stairs to the poop deck where the air had become colder and gustier. She held onto a rope running to a pinrail and turned her face into the cuffing wind.

The deck was tinged with yellow from the lanterns. The tiny flames created strange pillows of light in the fog. There were dark outlines of the watch crew in their positions waiting for orders from the wheel.

Captain Gibb and the first-mate were staring out over the port rail. The wind stole their words. Mac spotted Eva approaching. He dipped his head an inch and Gibb turned. He smiled a tight smile at her.

'Miss Eva. How do you feel about what the Grand Ocean has thrown at us for our last night?'

'Hello Captain. It's such a bleak haze.'

'True, but listen …' Captain Gibb said, and he stepped closer and pointed into the water. Eva blocked off the murmur of the party below, and the rumble of the wintry wind. What she heard coming from the ocean was the ship sluicing through the water,.

'Beautiful, isn't it?' the captain said.

'It's such a wonderful sound. I'll never forget it.'

'I'd guess,' Gibb said, and his eyes traced the outline of the sails and masts, 'that since noon we've had an easting of ten miles and a northing of five. I expect we'll be passing Cape Otway by dawn.' He glanced at the hatch over the cuddy. 'From what I hear, it seems everyone's enjoying your party below. It's been quite entertaining from up here.'

'It's going wonderfully and I'll compliment Giles for the food when I see him in the morning. Oh, and Father has broken the seal on the sherry cask and I believe he'll be bringing you a glass before he bungs it again.'

The flame illuminated Gibb's face, which stiffened a little.

'Miss Eva, send your father my thanks, but I'll not drink tonight. Or sleep. The next twenty-four hours are too important.'

Eva nodded. 'Of course, Captain. Well, I think he'll be up soon with the others anyway, to drink your toast, and that of your crew.'

CHAPTER NINETEEN

00.30 am Saturday 1 June
Eva

Much later, after the passengers had wobbled up the stairs to the deck and toasted the captain and crew, and after most had taken themselves to bed, and after the midnight bell, Eva was still on deck, and had convinced Raby to stay a few extra minutes.

'We may never be on the ocean again,' Eva said.

'It is beautiful,' Raby said. She had a scarf tied over her head to keep her hair from blowing about. 'But I'm so tired, Eva. Can we go to bed now?

So, they called goodnight to the captain and Mac. As she stepped below into the passageway, Eva heard Gibb call for another cast of the deep. She remembered something her father had told her – that these men who live on the sea were comparatively untroubled when they were a great distance from land or ice but when a coast was nearby they were more wary than even in the fiercest storm.

Eva almost turned to go back up to learn the result of the casting. But Raby tugged her arm.

'Come on Eva. Tomorrow will be a long day.'

CHAPTER TWENTY

Saturday 1 June
Eva

Eva could not sleep. The moody south-easterly assaulted the *Loch Ard*, making the ship tumble about in the swell and skate down the sides of waves.

On deck, the bell rang in four sets of two. Four o'clock in the morning. She rolled over, shuffled her pillow, pulled her blanket against the chill cabin air, and finally dozed.

She woke at a distant yell so dreadful she was convinced she must have had a nightmare.

Another yell. Boots pounded above the cabin.

When the bell rang again a minute later, it rang harshly – six doubles, eight doubles, ten. Eva lost count.

She took a moment to remind herself which bunk she was in before she sat up. Several times she'd found out the hard way against the ceiling.

She was in the bottom bunk and struggled out of bed to open the door. A night-lamp burned and sent the usual shadows along the passageway. With a shudder, the ship tilted then shifted sharply. The door thumped hard into Eva's back and made her gasp. She gripped the door frame to stop herself from falling into the passageway.

'What's happening?' Raby mumbled.

Mac's voice fired over the main deck. 'All hands! All hands!' The bell rang twins a half-dozen times more.

'I'll go look. It might be land,' Eva said. She pulled her dressing gown tight around her and struggled barefoot to the companionway.

Reginald Jones was hovering near the bottom of the steps and it sounded like he was weeping. Several other male passengers including Evory and Thomas ran past Eva up the steps. She pulled herself up behind them.

Sailors were running from their bunkrooms. Ran to pinrails. Shrouds. Hauled on lines.

Orders thundered from the poop. Haul into the wind! More sail! Unfurl topgallants! Hard to starboard!

Eva gripped the banister at the top of the companionway. What was happening?

The haze was clearing into patches of night. But the lanterns around the ship were enough to show everyone on deck that something vast and black was offset against the clearing, starry sky.

Eva's legs nearly buckled when she saw what the crew were looking at.

Fifty yards away, a rock cliff loomed like a massive tower. It was higher than the masts and it's edges disappeared into the night. It was not the soft misty Australia that should be in sight at dawn. This was something savage, and too close. How could it be real?

On the poop deck, the captain stood solid, watching.

'Now!' he roared 'Turn about!' His eyes leapt up the masts. They flicked out to port. His hand gesticulated hard sideways to someone up the mizzen.

Behind him, Mac and Baxter heaved on the wheel together. The ship turned harshly away from the rock and creaked and groaned with the strain of changed sails and the pressure of the rapid rudder change.

'Eva!' her father struggled to the top of the steps. He was vaguely dressed, with shirt but no collar. Jacket. Trousers. Socks, but no shoes.

'Father? What's happening?'

'I'll ask the captain. Your mother's with the girls. Go dress yourself then help her.'

Eva did not move. Then her father's eyes saw the black menace to port.

His voice became pebbles. 'Eva, go, now!'

At her cabin door, she could still hear the captain thundering orders forward and aloft. Inside, Raby had lit the lamp and was dressing.

She'd found her green velvet dress that she'd kept in the back of the wardrobe for the day they sighted land. Even as she tried to balance on the see-sawing floor, she was working the buttons on the lace collar. She had already put on her best shoes – the shoes she had long ago selected for her first steps in Australia. To find them, she had tossed all the other shoes from the under-seat storage onto the floor.

'Don't worry,' Raby said. 'I'll pack them after we've had a look at the new land. Are you going to dress or just stand there?' She tumbled against the wardrobe, laughed and passed Eva a pair of shoes from the floor. 'Put these on. I'll see you up on deck.'

Eva looked at Raby with confusion. 'Raby, it's …' The ship lurched and Eva and Raby collided. They snatched at the plank that edged the top bunk and Raby laughed again. The ship evened. Eva waited. She exhaled in relief.

She shook her head and realised she should not worry. The captain would sort it out like he always did and they'd soon be away from that black monster out there and on their approach to Melbourne. And if Raby's dress became covered in salt water before then, it would be her own fault.

After Raby left, Eva tugged the previous day's dress over her nightdress then slid on her jacket. She ignored the shoes Raby had given her, and pulled on her comfortable walking boots.

She opened the cabin door and heard the captain bellow something about anchors. The ship tilted again and a wave sent spray down the steps.

The anchors had not been out since the ship was in the Thames on their first night after the *Loch Ard* cast off. Why use anchors here?

Within a moment, the anchor chains began a prolonged vibrating judder along the ship. The *Loch Ard* lurched sideways and Eva tumbled to the cabin floor. The lamp extinguished itself. Voices in other cabins cried out.

She scrambled back onto her bed. Her fingers trailed over the patterned holes in the crochet of the blanket made by her grandmother long ago. Her heart pounded. This was not a normal storm. Should she check on her mother and the girls? Where had Raby gone? And how terrible of her to have left this mess so that Eva could barely move in the darkness.

Then, a tremendous, deafening crash shook everything. Eva did not need anyone to tell her that the sound was the steel hull driving along rock.

She was too shocked to get up. A minute or two later, the ship tipped away from the rock and floated free. How much damage? Was the *Loch Ard* strong enough? For the first time she wondered if an iron hull would be stronger than a wooden one.

But in the dark cabin she felt the swell of the ocean lift the ship and hurl it sideways against the rock again, smacking it as though it was a toy. Eva had never experienced violence like it in her life and it left her ears ringing and her body shaking.

From somewhere in the decks below there was an impossible sound.

Water gushing.

Then, in her cabin the glass in the porthole above the top bunk creaked then split.

Ocean spurted in like an icy, liquid flame and Eva fled blindly for her parents' cabin.

CHAPTER TWENTY-ONE

Saturday 1 June
Tom

It was around four in the morning and Tom had not slept for twenty-six hours. He stood on the deck feeling uneasy but with no idea why.

As the haze began to clear from white to dark grey, he realised the thing disturbing him was something he smelled, which was strange because the gusting wind made it difficult to smell anything.

He struggled to place the smell. It was a smell from his memory. And he could not work out why it bothered him.

Straz was on deck too, on the other side of the ship staring out into the black air. Immobile and watching. They had both stayed on deck with the rostered crew, deciding to wait for the fog to clear.

Then a bellow came from the bow and from the lookout and from the captain all in the same few seconds screaming to everyone that rock lay ahead. And Tom remembered what it was he could smell.

It was Australia.

He had smelled land. His land.

Then a huge black feature loomed up beside the ship. Mac rang the bell over and over and shouted for all hands. The ship creaked and turned. It heaved and jolted, moving away from the rock. But then its rear hull caught violently on underwater rocks. The noise was like the end of time. The

Loch Ard leaned away and seemed to rest for a few seconds. But the wind and waves were resting too, and suddenly they hurled the ship hard again.

Tom lost his footing and crashed to the deck. In a shocking, paralysing, blinding moment in his brain, everything in his life – the voyage, the ship, his family, his childhood, his future, which was just a moment ago normal and alright – suddenly became irreversibly and impossibly in peril.

Screams came from men and from the ship herself.

'We're holed!' someone howled, and at that moment Tom knew that any chance for the *Loch Ard* to escape out to sea was gone. The fog had cleared too late.

The ship tilted and Tom skidded on his back across the deck, crashing into the port rail. Above something creaked and snapped. A spar screeched along the rock face, snapped off the mast and fell.

A howl echoed from a tangle of sail and rigging on the deck.

'Help!'

Tom and Straz and a few other men crawled to the fallen spar. They tore away enough sail for the lamplights to show the face of the older able-seaman, Egan, half crushed on the deck.

Egan's head was barely visible and the spar was over his chest and pelvis and had wedged him against the mast.

Jimmy yelled at him. 'Can you move your legs?'

Egan shook his head. His eyes were wide with terror. Tom ducked as Egan's arms pushed in panic against the weight of the rigging that had come down with the spar.

The job was impossible. The men struggled against the angle and motion of the ship. They tugged the sail foot by foot until it finally untangled from Egan. Waves began to pour over the deck then an unbelievable roar made Tom look up as a huge wave rose cold and dark like a train engine and crashed angrily on top of everyone and everything. It threw three or four crew over the rail, arms grabbing for anything to hold. Legs running in the air, screams, then gone.

Then Mac yelled. 'Pearce! You and those men! Get the starboard lifeboat onto its davits!'

On the poop deck, the captain was urging two women, who had somehow found lifebelts, down towards the lifeboat.

'The boat's for the women,' Egan yelled at Tom, 'and children.' His voice was weakening. 'Go get them off. You can come back for me.' But he knew. He shut his eyes and let the men scramble away from him. Two minutes later the sea took the spar and Egan.

Tom fought with the men to untangle the ropes that secured the pulleys. The lifeboat had to be raised from its skid before it could be lowered into the ocean. He heard yelling from the port side of the ship that was being crashed against the rock wall. When he glanced over, the lanterns showed the determined faces of passengers Pitt, Mitchell and even Jones, and the two Carmichael boys all fighting to unfasten the other lifeboat. For a moment pride and horror knotted inside Tom. With rock so close to port, that boat was unlikely to get into the sea.

But the captain had ordered Tom and the others to release the starboard lifeboat and in truth it was the only one they could possibly free.

Someone yelled from beside Tom, 'If we tether it to the mast, then release it, we might get the women in it from a wet deck!'

It was the only way. The air was filled with thunderous waves and the evil baying wind. Spray made hands and feet slip and wasted their precious energy. Every wave flooded the deck now. Every surge of ocean felt like it had begun in the freezing Antarctic. It threw the men at deckhouses and masts and they yelled in pain but fought back to free the lifeboat.

Again, the ocean tipped the ship precariously up then back, shredding more of the hull below. The hencoop snapped from its bolts and bounced into the ocean as though it was a rock being skimmed on a pond's surface. The rooster, the only creature spared the knife, flew from its now-open base and flapped and squawked bloody murder, once, and was gone.

Tom turned to see a monstrous surf as tall as a barn heave from the stern, up and over the poop deck. It punched the men from the wheel, and slammed into the two older Carmichael girls who were hugging the banister on the steps below the poop. The wave flung them, screaming, into the frothy darkness. Captain Gibb had jammed himself against the mizzen mast but it was clear that, if another wave like that came soon, he also would be gone.

Tom hoped … if the wave had thrown the girls clear of the ship; if … they had not landed on rock or someone else or debris; if … their lifebelts were properly tied on; if … the girls were conscious now, they may be able to struggle onto an item washed overboard and make their way to whatever shore there might be nearby.

Someone's knife finally sliced the final rope holding the lifeboat, but a surge of the Grand Ocean swelled to six feet over the deck and crashed like it was concrete. It snatched the lifeboat, and Tom and Straz, and the men with them, and took them all.

CHAPTER TWENTY-TWO

Saturday 1 June
Eva

Eva and the rest of the family knew their mother demanded order. Mrs Carmichael would hang her clothes in her wardrobe according to colour, and then according to how they matched her shoes. She trained all her children to respect their belongings. How to use saucers and coasters so cups did not leave rings on furniture. How to keep their jackets well brushed and their shoes polished.

Eva struggled to her parents' cabin. The door swung open and shut on its hinges. A candle lit the room from inside a storm lantern swinging from a hook. Her father had returned with lifebelts. The cabin was crammed with him, her mother, Raby, Margaret and Annie, all fighting against the writing desk that had been thoroughly tethered to the wall during the voyage but had now broken free. The doctor's foot was wedged against one leg to hold it in place and he was spitting angry words at the cords of a dusty lifebelt he was trying to fit onto his wife. Annie was on the floor amongst feet and blankets, in another fit and frothing from her mouth. Raby wore a chunky lifebelt around her chest. She stood there pale, grasping the edge of the top bunk. Margaret held onto her tightly around her waist and sobbed into her belly.

'Eva! Up there … it's so terrible!' Raby said, half comforting Margaret with empty pats.

Their mother straightened up. 'And I can hear water below.' Her voice vibrated in a high pitch. 'I hope none has reached our crates. All our clothes and linen. Everything will be ruined.'

'Eva,' her father said thickly. He shoved a lifebelt at her. 'Put this on now.'

Eva looked at him and it felt like she had never seen him before. His battle to get the knots untied and the lifebelt onto his wife was failing, but something in his eyes showed a realisation that giving her a lifebelt was as useful as handing her a cupcake.

He had given Eva the last good lifebelt. None for him.

The ship creaked then jolted violently, tossing them all back against Raby and Margaret. Annie slid across the floor and rolled foetally in a corner. There was no point trying to get her to stand until the fit was over.

'Raby. Eva,' their father ordered. 'Both of you get up on deck. If they've got the first lifeboat ready, get yourselves in. We'll,' and he hesitated just long enough that it seemed he might not believe his own words. 'We'll get in the next one and see you on shore.'

When he said, "on shore" it sounded like he was picturing a gentle row in at sunrise to a soft, tranquil beach far from fog and wind and waves. But the tearing of the hull reached further aft now, and the porthole in their cabin cracked loudly. Water leaked in, not as powerfully as it did in Eva and Raby's cabin, but it spilled onto the top bunk, and soaked into the bedding.

Their mother was in her own world. She moaned, 'Oh, how will we get all these blankets dry in this weather!'

'Go now, girls!' their father said with a deep croaking passion Eva had never heard from him before. He gave up on the strings and pressed his hands quickly on each girl's cheeks then flapped a hand as though he was waving a puppy away. 'Go!'

'Father! Mother?' Raby begged.

'It's alright dear,' their mother answered. 'We'll be right behind you. Annie will be clear of this in a moment.' The screech of the ship and Margaret's escalating screams competed with her last words.

Raby and Eva staggered along the passageway, now black entirely. They bumped past two men who gave way to them. They struggled up the steps, then a lurch of the deck almost sent them back down. Eva pulled herself up and looked across the vaguely lit deck. The lifeboats were not out at all. She turned to the poop deck.

'We'll ask Captain Gibb!' Raby yelled.

CHAPTER TWENTY-THREE

Pre-dawn, Saturday 1 June
13 weeks after leaving Gravesend
Tom

The first part of Tom to hit the water was the side of his head, and excruciating pain exploded inside his ear. Then instant cold encased him entirely.

Instinctively, he swam down into the tangle of ocean and fought through the debris to get away from the ship. The water sucked and churned him. It almost snapped him in two. He struggled to the surface but before he'd drawn half a breath a tongue of surf slammed onto him tearing and tumbling him as though he was a piece of driftwood.

Under water, anger rose. It knotted with fear. It crossed his mind that he might lose this fight. But he had to survive, for his mother and sisters and young brother. His future. He could not drown.

Something heavy crashed into him. It was clothed. A human. It slid away and Tom swam hard and prayed he was swimming upwards. He tried to kick his boots off but they were knotted tight and jammed onto his feet.

It took almost too long to get night air into his lungs.

When he did, a soul groaned to his right. Frantic splashing of someone struggling to stay afloat. When the groan uttered again, it was the voice of the first-mate.

'Mac!'

The ocean shoved them underneath side by side.

Mac's voice gurgled as his head shot from the water. 'Pearce! Help … get … coat off.'

Tom heaved in a breath, submerged and blindly fought Mac's coat buttons open. The water sucked the coat away.

Tom surfaced and yelled, 'The lifeboat's around here sir!'

'Don't want … lifeboat!' Mac shouted. 'Need … to get on board.'

'She's sinking, sir.'

The night was wind and waves and screams.

'Need to get back.' Mac sputtered. 'The captain.'

The captain goes down with his ship. But the first-mate did not need to go down with the *Loch Ard*. Mac seemed to have decided otherwise. Someone was shouting nearby but Tom grabbed at ropes and kicked at boxes until he had shoved Mac closer to the ship. Mac snatched onto rigging that hung from the fallen mizzen mast.

Only one of Tom's ears was working. There were more shouts and cries for help. They seemed to come from every direction.

'Get away Pearce!' Mac yelled. A silhouette. 'Save yourself and anyone you can.'

Tom obeyed. A sob rose inside him and made him cough. He swam many hard strokes that only carried him a dozen or so yards from the last bit of light filtering from a lantern bolted to a mast. He turned and looked.

The iron ship howled. It broke somewhere and some of it grazed slowly down the rocks and sent sparks along the cliff that, for seconds, illuminated her fall. Huge rivets launched like dozens of gunshots. The sea surged. The hull scraped along many yards of its length. The screech of metal was deafening. The top masts cracked against the cliff, snapped like twigs, and folded in a slow, wailing motion towards the deck. The last lantern expired. For a moment, there was silence. Then terrible cries for help came from places Tom could not see.

He felt the water go over his head. It numbed his face. He rested from his fight to surface. It was a relief not to swim. The cold had reached his bones. Calmness swamped him. He could sleep now.

Sodden sail draped onto him. He stirred.

A demand to live.

He jabbed his legs down and up. His arms strained at the ocean. He burst to the surface and breathed air.

It felt like hours had passed since the ship had hit the rock. But, when he thought how many times he'd fought for each breath, it was probably no more than ten minutes since that wave had punched him into the sea.

He forced a stroke at swimming, and another, and swam into the dark towards what might be some form of land.

He swam into ropes and sails, and fought them away. Scraps of wood and cargo bruised and scraped his arms and back and head ... and he swam into something squishy that turned out to be a blanket. He tried to float on his back to rest himself, but the fight and tumble of the waves spun him like a cork. Then a wave crashed another person into him. The body smelled of blood – lots of it. He grabbed the person's collar and his fingers felt a kerchief at the neck. A silk kerchief.

'Straz!' Tom tugged on Robert Strasenburgh's hair to keep his friend's face turned up. Something slithered into Tom's neck. An arm? Another person. With his boots on he could not hold a third person on the surface. But then he found that the thing was not human, but a thick rope that should be hanging neatly coiled at the pinrails but was now tangling Straz and himself.

His friend was sliding down. 'Straz!'

A wave ripped Straz's hair from Tom's hand but he snatched out again and caught hold of the kerchief at the back of Straz's neck.

'Straak …' Seawater choked him. He spewed it out and it was a moment before he realised the only thing in his hand was the kerchief. He dived. He fought at objects and ropes.

But the ocean had torn Straz away and Tom howled under water and heard his own bubbling voice. All he could do was save himself. He rose for air then slid under the surging waves that sucked at him. He fought at the tangle of rope. It slid off as though he was removing trousers.

And he swam.

CHAPTER TWENTY-FOUR

Saturday 1 June
Eva

'Oh, ladies!' Gibb yelled down at them from the poop deck. 'I pray for God's sake you get off this ship and safely to shore!'

Eva and Raby could barely hold the banister.

'Please,' he begged. He struggled to keep his hold on the rail. 'Get word to my wife that I stayed by my post just as a captain should, right to the end.' These words fell like boulders from him. The words almost paralysed Eva. Gibb was saying goodbye.

'Captain Gibb!' Raby called. 'You'll save us, I know!'

'Get to the lifeboat,' Gibb ordered, pointing starboard. 'They'll have it right soon.' Lantern light showed huge disappointment in his face. 'I'm sorry,' he mouthed.

A great sadness grew in Eva's chest as she thought of Gibb's wife, whoever she was. Once, just a week or so before, Eva had seen Gibb pull a photograph out of his jacket pocket and look longingly at it.

She gripped Raby's arm and tugged her and they clung, terrified, together near the companionway, watching the men straining to dislodge the lifeboat. Other passengers clambered up from below. None were Carmichaels.

Raby screamed and, when Eva followed her horrified look, a wave had risen high over the stern. Before they could even take a breath, the wave slammed a ten-foot wall onto the poop deck, and hurled the girls hard into the starboard rail. Pain shot through Eva's hip and ribs. Then the wave lifted them both high and dumped them into the sea.

Blackness. Sleep. Awake. Freezing water swallowing her.

Her grip on Raby's sleeve became her own desperate fingers snatching at the ocean.

When her lifebelt forced her, gasping, to the surface, all was darkness except two pale lanterns on the masts a dozen impossible yards away. The starlight dangled so peacefully above as though it was a whole other world from the howl and vision of the heartbreak in this tiny corner of the earth.

Salt stung Eva's eyes and burned her throat.

Someone yelled. 'Help me!' Other voices too far away.

None sounded like Raby. She called to her, but no one answered.

She wondered why her skin was on fire. Strangely, it was the sting of the freezing sea. The surge hurled her again, backwards.

Confusion. Noise. Water.

Waves lifted her and smacked into her, and the wind whipped the sea at her face. Her hair tangled around her neck, and into her eyes and mouth. Her arms and legs fought against the water that despite the lifebelt, tried to suck her downwards, then she rose and gulped for air. She forced herself to think what her brother William would do, then knew she should only try to inhale when her face felt the cold of the wind. So when cold air blew on one of her cheeks, she gulped air, and when it did not, she waited. In her head, she wept a prayer asking God to teach her how to swim. She had to find her family.

Although the lifebelt kept her head mostly above the water, it also forced up into her face and gave her another battle she had not expected. Then one of the cords snapped, which left just two.

Objects large, small or tangled spat from the ship and a great shadow of a box tumbled ahead of her. She kicked out and caught the wire door of the hencoop. The wire tore skin from her fingers and the scraping made her cry in pain and she let go.

'Wait!' she called to the coop and for a stupid moment wondered where the rooster had gone. She had to find a better grip. The coop bounced away but Eva kicked against something and launched forward enough to snatch at the frame and, finally, she had it. There was enough wood in the coop for it to float, but she sensed it would not last.

'Thank God!' But where was Raby? 'Raby, Raby! Are you safe? I've found the hencoop. Follow my voice and swim to me. Raby!'

The gale answered. Then a man's voice.

'Is that you Miss Eva?'

'Mr Mitchell?'

'Keep calling and I'll come to you!' he yelled. He must have swallowed too much water because the words gurgled from him in a voice that reminded Eva of one of her father's patients who came one day to the Carmichael surgery for medicine to heal an infected boil in his throat.

'I'm here! I'm here!' She called. Then the other side of the hencoop pulled down. Somewhere, voices cried out. Mostly men but a woman too although Eva could not tell who. She called again and again, but the wind sucked her words away.

Furious splashing approached from Eva's left and another voice.

'Miss Carmichael!'

It was Jones' voice, and he and Art Mitchell hung onto the coop with Eva, and she knew it could not hold together much longer.

'Where's Miss Raby?' Art Mitchell asked. 'And your family?' he added.

'I don't know,' Eva cried back. 'Please help me find them?' But she knew … these two men and herself could barely hold themselves afloat, let alone search for others. The coop creaked and cracked. It was surrendering to the power of the waves and its corners were seesawing under the weight of the three.

Eva called out again for her sister. Her mother. Her father. They may have found boxes or might even be in a lifeboat, coming to rescue them.

'Miss Carmichael,' Jones said. He came, hand over hand, around the coop until he was close beside her. His feet were struggling under the water and they kicked Eva's shins several times but he did not seem to notice. Whatever he'd been about to say to her was swamped by a surge and they all returned to the surface coughing and gasping for breath.

Art Mitchell was close to Eva and, when she was thrown against him, she noticed he wore a lifebelt. And Jones had something, a flotation ring perhaps, circled around his chest.

Something powerful burst up from below, right beside Eva and so close that she lost her hold on the coop. It splashed down, landing heavily just two feet from her. A spar from the ship that could have just killed them but now could keep them alive. Eva turned and threw her arms and chest over it. Mitchell and Jones followed her just as the hencoop collapsed and a wave hurled it at them, dashing wood and wire into their heads and bodies.

Once, as a child, Eva had lost her way in a snowstorm. Even then, she had not been as cold as she was now in the wintery ocean where her limbs were almost entirely numb.

Fear magnified the chill. Where were the others? Why was no lifeboat there with men pulling them from the water?

The murderous mist parted again and the stars dripped just enough light to show the outlines of blacks and greys. On the ship, a lantern was still alight near the wheelhouse. A silhouette slid across the light then fell. A wave crashed over the deck and smashed out the tiny flame. Then a long screeching noise sliced the night.

'What's that?' Mitchell yelled.

'The ship splitting open,' Jones said flatly, as though he had completely expected it, which he had.

Things pinged onto the cliff and rocks, lighting up like fire crackers. Then the ocean spoke in its own voice. Suction, like a giant slurping his soup.

'So, it's truly over,' Eva eventually whispered.

For an eerie minute, the wind eased and the pattern of waves paused. They stared towards the upper part of the ship hanging there.

The main deck must be on a ledge of underwater rock. Black shapes hugged the deck rail and masts. They howled and screamed into the violence of the weather. But the newly scrubbed deck, and newly painted fittings, and newly tarred shrouds all followed the tilt, screeching towards the water. The tall black shapes of the remaining masts shortened until they stopped with perhaps a quarter of their height visible. The *Loch Ard*, which had appeared so huge on the Town Pier at Gravesend three months earlier, was all but gone.

They had been in the water for nearly an hour. The distant voices gradually became fewer, and then none. Eva called when she could get her breath but it was just the three of them and the tossing and roar of the waves. They did not talk. They clung to the spar freezing towards sleep.

Numbness chewed at her. Did her mother and father escape? Margaret and Annie? Or were they still in their cabin when the hull ripped away? She could not bear to picture it. And where were the others? Surely Thomas had survived, and Raby, and Evory.

CHAPTER TWENTY-FIVE

Pre-dawn, Saturday 1 June
The Loch Ard

In the moments after Raby and Eva fled their cabin, in the depths of the ocean below, a ledge of underwater rock tore along half-a-dozen sheets of iron hull-plate at the *Loch Ard's* port rear, shredding it as though it was peeling layers off a cabbage.

Along the keel, the side plates buckled, butt straps snapped, liners ripped, iron mouldings sighed then folded.

In the hold, a family of rats that had mostly managed to stay hidden now skittered along the internal framework in furious lines heading towards the upper deck and onto anything that would float.

In the deck below George Gibb's cabin, freezing water entered the ship. Its entrance began slowly because this section of the pitch-black hold was crammed with cargo of ceramic tiles and spare mast parts. Then the *Loch Ard* tilted violently and the cargo shifted enough for the leak to become a spout, then a flood.

Further forward in the hold, the large supply of railway irons moved a few inches to port then the ship trembled sideways and grated angrily against the rock wall. Above deck, the masts and yards behaved like fire-steels on the rock and shot angry sparks into the air. Further forward, the steam donkey-engine broke its bolts and crashed down through the decks. The shift of weight in the hold snapped the lashings securing the railway irons, followed by the cables that held in place dozens of barrels of dry, then wet, cement.

The sailors stopped fighting to save the ship and now each man fought for his own life although a few looked about to try to save another. Some fled up shrouds doing their best to stay above the ocean. Mac held the ship's wheel because it was all he could do, then a wave smashed over him and hurled him ten yards into the sea.

Evory and Thomas Carmichael had tried to help with a lifeboat but abandoned it when it became impossible. They saw the wave wash their older sisters away. They saw the captain order men to try to save them – 'Ropes! Life buoys!' Now Thomas and Evory were together at the base of the foremast clutching each other and holding on to anything they could. A huge swell snatched them, tumbled them against a railing, against numerous solid objects and into the sea. They were lost to each other. Thomas choked, inhaled seawater, and was gone. Evory gasped to the surface. He stayed afloat for a long ten minutes, watching the ship in the ghostly light of a lantern light glowing on a mast. People called out about him. They struggled for each other, and someone, a crewman, grasped at Evory's clothes. Evory fought him off. He battled for every breath. He rested a moment and saw the orange glow of the lantern like a stain on water. He watched some fish school above him. He saw Jules Verne's world under the sea and closed his eyes.

The swell shifted the ship. Rivet heads shot from the hull. More plating peeled away. The rock hooked under the top deck and the weight of water and loose goods tugged at the hull. The *Loch Ard*'s frame opened up like a can having its lid removed and she spilled her insides into the ocean and to the other floor of the world.

Crates of umbrellas. Scissors. Lead shot. Rolls of zinc. Copper plating. Mrs Carmichael and Margaret. They floated off the ship; clutched at the life buoys and boxes, but things tangled around them and pulled them down. They stopped fighting and one by one their hands relaxed and they slept.

What could float from the ship popped to the surface. Furniture; barrels with more air than contents. Sails, rigging and spare or broken spars.

The proud bowsprit tilted down and men skidded along the deck clamouring for anything they could hold. Crashing into fittings; each other. Many screamed. Some begged for their mothers.

Eventually, under the water, the *Loch Ard* split into two sections and the lower slid down to join the cargo, tearing the bow from the main deck. The hull, bow first, descended almost gracefully the twenty yards to the sea floor. Its bowsprit glided so gently that its last movement as it grated to a stop on coral and rock and weed and sand was to slide forwards on the gritty ground and under the edge of a huge slab of rock. On the surface, jammed for now on the bottom of the cliff, clung the remains of the main deck.

One section of deck that did not break apart was the poop. After Tom helped Mac pull himself back on board, Mac crawled across the deck and discovered Gibb unconscious, his skull smashed. Broken-hearted, Mac knew the captain could not be saved. He knew too that Gibb was a man who would go down with his ship unless everyone was rescued first. As the main deck began to creak and tilt off the rock, Mac hauled Gibb to the wheel. Fiercely he forced rope around the captain's back, under his armpits and through the useless wheel. Then he jammed his own hands into the ropes. The water was already at his chest. He said a silent goodbye to his wife and children, each by name. He prayed for them in his heart.

CHAPTER TWENTY-SIX

Saturday 1 June
Eva

The ocean diluted Eva's sense of time. Was it barely an hour ago that her father had shoved the lifebelt at her? Surely dawn would come soon so they could see the other survivors.

The waves had tossed each of the three off the spar at different times but they had helped each other back on.

'I'm so cold,' Art Mitchell muttered. He had been shivering violently for too long. 'Save me from this terrible sea!' he sobbed. 'Please!'

Eva would have given him her jacket if she could. But the lifebelt and her fading efforts to hold on to the rolling spar, made it impossible.

Jones, the man who had spent three months keeping himself away from the edges of the ship, now worked his rubber life-ring up over his shoulders and head, an action that took him underwater several times and used up vital strength. He gasped when he realised how difficult it would be to stay afloat without its help. He hooked an arm over the spar then pressed the ring over Mitchell's head who now had two floating aids on him.

Mitchell said nothing. He did not argue that Jones should keep the device that might save his life. This man Mitchell, who had whispered love to Raby, was now out of his depth in so many ways.

'There's surf breaking somewhere that way,' Jones said, waving a dark arm towards a rim of rock. 'It might mean a beach we can get to.'

'Oh!' Eva said. 'I could not swim that far! I barely made it from the hencoop to the spar.'

'Art?' Jones asked.

Eva felt two things happen. Something primal and unspoken was communicated between the men. Then the spar rolled and rose higher in the water, and Eva discovered she was the only person attached it.

'Miss Carmichael!' Jones called from a few yards away. 'Please hang on. If there's a beach, we'll find a way to get back to you! But I hope and pray a lifeboat gets to you first.'

Eva could not answer. A loneliness soaked into her that could not pass her lips.

She heard splashing of arms. The dark balls that were the men's heads rose then fell behind a swell and were gone. Her lifebelt chose that moment to float too well and she sensed her body slipping down through it. The spar rolled away out of reach. How strange, she thought, to drown inside a lifebelt.

As the icy southern water salted her lungs and grasped at her life, she knew there would be no boats and only she could save her life now.

'God,' she whispered again at the vibrant sky. 'You need to teach me to swim.'

She found the spar, then kicked hard at each of her numb feet until she had forced off her boots, so grateful that she had not had time to tie them on. The sensation of bare feet in the water roused her and her instinct grew to keep kicking.

Then Eva remembered their red setter, Ferdinand, swimming after ducks in the deep end of the pond one sunny afternoon a year ago. Eva had giggled at the craziness of her dog's style – all four legs scrambling madly in the water, and a smirk on his face – so now she loosened her hold on the spar and flailed her arms and legs in a Ferdinand way. She fought the surf that sucked her under water. Whenever the lifebelt jolted her to the surface, she tilted her head back at the sky and gasped for air. The swimming gave her hope, but it exhausted her.

Every now and then she called out but no one answered. Her voice was lost to the sound of dark wind and waves. Her words croaked from salty thirst and from desperate sadness. But except for a swathe of bruises, she was uninjured and it gave her hope she could survive. If only daylight would come and wash away the grey darkness, but it was winter here with its long nights and short days.

Swimming was hard enough but more and more Eva had to fend off cargo that battered at her. After a few minutes, she managed to get her arms around a small bobbing barrel.

She rested and listened. There was surf, but it was not in the direction that Jones and Mitchell had swum.

If she could reach some rocks, and if getting onto them did not kill her, she might be able to wait until the sun rose to see how to get to safety but she knew the light would also show her things she did not want to see.

CHAPTER TWENTY-SEVEN

Saturday 1 June
Tom

Something solid stabbed into Tom's hip and jolted him awake. He was half out of the water and could not feel his arms.

A cold blast of wind blew over his back. It bit through his clothes and into his flesh. He raised his head and stared, blinking. The pre-dawn sky dripped grey light and he realised his body was draped over an overturned lifeboat. His hands were out in front of him gripping a thick loop of rope.

The ocean swelled from below and his aching ribs grated over the planks.

'Hoi!' Tom shouted. 'Anyone there?' But the wind and waves ate his words.

No human sound answered and he doubted he'd hear them anyway with the smashing of water onto rocks and objects. But how could he possibly be alone?

He crawled up with his knees and finally relieved the angle of his shoulders. Precious blood pumped along his arms, tingling to start with, then like lightning bolts paining him enough that he almost let go. The ocean surged up under the boat and threatened to roll the whole thing but it dropped away before it did.

Black rock towered around him and each wave that struck the rock exploded into a deafening upsurge that subsided a moment before it erupted again. Against one cliff, the tops of two of the *Loch Ard*'s masts scraped the rock. They stuck out of the sea and nudged back and forth with the waves.

Above the ruin of the ship, the cliff rose eighty feet or more. Other dark cliffs swept off at angles then disappeared. Beyond any or all might be blind corners, or more cliffs. Or perhaps, almost outside hope, a beach. But then what? All he could recall of this part of Victoria's coastline was that it was mostly uninhabited.

If a wrecked ship was not the backdrop of this corner of the coast, Tom and his school friends might have looked at the water and savoured the challenge. They could try to dive deep enough to see the bottom. They could learn to ride the waves with their bodies. The Yarra had offered not much more than mud and crabs and random sightings of sharks.

The thought of sharks filled Tom with sudden panic then something careened into his thighs and sent a blaze of agony through his legs and pelvis. He jerked his head to see what had hit him and it was a wooden table, about three feet long and right side up. Not a shark.

A wave sucked the table away and he had no strength to reach it. Everywhere he looked, long snakes of rope and half-submerged clouds of sails tangled around cargo. Bodies too.

'I can't,' Tom whispered. 'I'm not strong enough.' But then he remembered his uncle.

Tom was fourteen when his father died while away on a job in New Zealand. The news overwhelmed Tom. Furious with grief, he fled the house the afternoon before the memorial service. His Uncle Edgar found him at dusk at a small pier on the edge of the Yarra and sat on the boards beside him. Neither spoke for ages.

'I can't,' Tom finally said, whispering so he did not weep.

Uncle Edgar let the words rest for a minute.

'Your mother needs you,' Uncle Edgar said quietly. 'You're her eldest son. The man of her house now.'

'I can't even survive the church service. I'm not strong enough.'

'Right now,' and Uncle Edgar's eyes trailed a small fishing boat being rowed past, 'you don't need to get through tomorrow. For now, all you need to do is get through the five minutes it'll take us to walk to the road. Then the next five to get home. In the morning, you only have to get through breakfast. Then through the taxi ride to the church. And, even there, you only have to get through the first hymn. Then listen to one part at a time of the service. When it's over, five minutes at a time, you'd have stood at your mother's side and helped her through it all, and have been an example to your siblings.'

A light had lit in Tom. And he did it all by telling himself over and over that he only had to survive the next five minutes. And the next.

Tom looked around at the sea. He'd do another five minutes of it. All he had to do now was decide what to swim towards.

A smaller wave knocked the table into him again, as though reminding him of its presence. Tom inhaled and shoved away from the lifeboat, and hauled his chest onto the table top.

A swell powered up from below and dumped him back into the ocean. He struggled to the surface and heaved in air. The table had vaulted away but he swam four exhausted strokes and pulled himself onto it again. This time he prepared for the surge and balanced his body, half on the table, half in the water, steering with his boots and wishing they were not tied tightly on his feet.

The ocean surged again. Roared. Echoed. The waves and wind wailed through holes in the cliff, or was it the wailing of voices? Only one of his ears worked and he could not tell.

The swell moved him forward. Backward. Forward. After perhaps a quarter of an hour, it had nudged him into a gap between two cliffs. The pre-dawn light showed him a grey glimpse of lighter coloured surf. And the belt of a pale beach.

A beach. Just there. Yet it may as well be a hundred miles away.

Five minutes.

Another set of waves tossed chests and furniture at him that the dying ship was still ejecting, as if the poor beast had entirely opened up below the water and freed all her lighter cargo. More tangles of rope, and long strands of slimy kelp swept around him. Almost weeping, he screamed at them and kicked them away. No other humans called out.

The waves seemed to have direction, like they wanted to reach shore too, so slowly Tom kicked and surfed, and steered himself and the table towards the gap again.

A corner of the beach opened then vanished. When he saw it again, it sat waiting at the end of a deep, dark limestone canyon. Then the table caught on something hard and almost hurled him off but he fought back onto it.

Another wave bounced him forward a little further.

Were others from the *Loch Ard* already on that beach?

'Come on!' he growled to himself.

But the battle was inside him now. He was exhausted. Famished. Terribly thirsty. And the bruises and cold sent pain through him that burned and froze him at the same time.

Then a huge swell thrust Tom and the table up in a frightening arc and threw him far forward to within twenty yards of the beach. The moment of thrill vanished as the swell dropped him onto a rocky outcrop. The rock under the surface of the water grated the edge of the table and tore the skin from his knuckles. Before he could yell, another wave tossed him entirely into the water and he sank, and his boots made the glorious discovery that he had touched the sea floor.

When he kicked back to the surface the table had got itself stuck in a tangle of cargo. Another swell lifted Tom, hurling him sideways towards rocks on his left but the water fell and sucked him out again. The next three waves nudged him closer to the beach. He swam with them, fighting. He had to.

His boots touched ground again and he could almost walk. As his chest rose from the water, the wind stung through his clothes.

The water's edge now showed its horror. Organic shapes of bodies tumbled and rolled amongst the dark shapes of broken furniture and cargo. Tom knew he would recognise each person so he didn't look. They were dead and he was alive and an appalling guilt rose in him. He caught a glimpse of a body floating a couple of yards away. It's legs were missing from the knees down, perhaps sliced by a falling yard, or a knotted rope. Nausea rose in him and he focused on a clear slice of shore.

Then the ocean rolled a solid wave and sent him sprawling into the shallows. The undertow sucked at him and dragged his face along sand and shells and forced grit into his mouth and nose and clothes. It grazed his cheeks and dragged him back towards the sea.

He fought forward until he could stand, but his legs had no strength and he collapsed to his knees and crawled from the water. Every inch was a miracle. Each grain of sand and broken shell under his bleeding hands was like a tiny glow from heaven. He crawled between debris and bodies until he was clear of the water. And he did not stop until he reached soft, dry sand that told him he was past the high-tide line, then he vomited.

The last thing Tom felt was his cheek and forehead thwacking the sand as he collapsed into unconsciousness.

CHAPTER TWENTY-EIGHT

Dawn, Saturday 1 June
Tom

A gull screeched.

Tom ignored it. It screeched again and it sounded human, but why would a gull sound like a person?

He opened an eye and noticed the sky was lighter. He had probably only been unconscious for twenty or so minutes. The air blew harshly over his wet clothes. He was shivering uncontrollably. Sand and sharp shells pressed into his cheek.

The gull screeched again.

Another person! Tom forced himself onto his knees, then onto his unsteady legs. His eyes traced the water and along the edge of the half-lit canyon of ocean and cliffs. Something moved against distant rocks. It waved. An arm and a scream – definitely not a gull.

He rubbed his eyes, burning from the salt and wind. In the war he had just fled, a person was out there, perhaps thirty yards from the water's edge. An awakening pumped through his mind and body. But he hesitated. The odds were against him. If he went out, they could both be lost.

The thought did not hover long and it shamed him it had even crossed his mind.

He dropped to the sand and fought each boot from his feet, cursing his habit of tying double knots. He stripped off his jacket and found himself, implausibly, wading into the ocean he had just fled. Between each wave, the undertow sucked him further from the beach, and he let it until he was forced to swim. It was a woman out there, who was only afloat because she wore the remains of a lifebelt. Frighteningly, it took just minutes to reach her, half-draped over a box. In the few minutes it had taken him to reach her, she had passed out.

'Ma'am,' he yelled. Her head flopped about in the water. Her loosened hair covered her face. She could be any one of the women on board but she was the right size to be one of the older Carmichael daughters.

'Miss!' A wave crashed over them and scraped and rolled their bodies along the rocks. He tried to raise her face. 'Wake up! Wake up Miss!'

For the first time since he had woken on the upturned lifeboat, he remembered that Straz had drowned and for a moment grief blinded him.

Then the ocean smashed them again. He held the woman against the box. She spluttered and gasped for breath and a wave washed her hair from her face. It was Miss Eva. Tom took a quick look around but there were no other of her family.

'Miss Eva!' She stirred again and another wave swamped them and she faded. The frozen wind bit into Tom's face.

A broken ale cask vaulted towards him. It had a binding of rope still attached and his fingers snagged it just in time. Nothing was in the cask except water and weed. He tipped it over and trapped air inside and it gave enough buoyancy to hold him and let him rest briefly. The girl stirred again.

Then, as though a joke was needed, the rooster teetered past, his feet curled tight in the air and his proud neck broken and swaying under its carcass in the water.

Tom's eyes measured the canyon. Their position and the angle they needed was not as good as when he had been on the table on his earlier battle to shore.

'Oh, please … get me out!' Miss Eva begged in a burst. 'I'm so cold.' Her lips were blue. Voice thin. Body trembling.

'We're going to swim to the beach,' Tom said. 'Kick with your feet.'

Her eyes opened. Tom read the words that came to her lips. 'A beach?'

'It's not far!' he said even though it felt like a world away. 'Come on. We can do it together.'

He let go of the cask. Ahead, the tangles of furniture and ship's fixings were beginning to choke the canyon.

'Take my hand! Swim with your other. I'll find something else to help us!'

Eva obeyed. Tom reached for a tea chest but it bounced away from him. A smart wooden chair tumbled to his right and he managed to grasp a timber of the back support. The cushion was Indian rubber and it helped the chair stay afloat.

'Kick your legs,' he told her. But she was waning. He heaved the chair around in front of them.

'Hold tight!' He pressed one of her hands forward, making her grasp the chair's back. She nodded faintly like she understood. Tom looked over his shoulder and waited for a swell of waves to break behind them. 'Hang on Miss Eva.'

When it rose under them and the power tried to drag them apart, Tom pulled the girl closer than he would ever have dared on any other day and steered them on the blast of water. The beach came closer, and the surge dragged them through twisted mats of crates and ropes and broken luggage. Tom shoved and kicked at everything that threatened to tangle them, then the water suctioned them out again.

'Hang on!' Another wave carried them into the canyon.

A flash of memory rolled over Tom. He was running a race at school. He was winning, then his pal George Lyon gained and began to pass. Tom threw himself harder. The grass was dry and warm under his bare feet. His toes dug in. His legs pumped. Left. Right. His calves burned. His lungs wanted to burst.

Bored students on the sidelines began to look up, stand up, cheer for one boy or the other. On the second lap, Tom gained a stride ahead of George. He held it for a few yards until George passed him again. The finish line was still half a lap away and now the race became a battle. Over his own wheezing for air, Tom could hear George breathing hard. Then, about three yards before the sandy line in the grass, Tom inched to the lead and held it to win. He let his pace slow naturally. Behind him came the thud-thud of George's feet and then the feet of the other six boys in the race, like a wave reaching the shore. Tom had won, for the first time ever.

In the ocean that never rested, they were only eight or nine yards from the shore. If he had been alone, he could make it, but he had a girl and a chair. And this was his second lap.

'We're nearly there. Do you see the sand?' he said struggling to talk now.

She peered through her wild hair. If he let go of her, she would simply slip away. He thought he saw her nod.

Tom unfurled her fingers from the chair leg. 'We have to swim without the chair. Do you hear me?' She did not respond.

A rebounding wave slapped them both in the face. Miss Eva gasped and her eyes opened wide. The chair tumbled away. A piece of broken spar jolted into Tom's shoulder and the pain paralysed him for a moment.

'Come on!' he yelled, angry now at the world. 'Ready?' He was going even if she was not. 'One!' He kicked out and swung an arm in a strong stroke. And he felt her body respond weakly beside his.

'And, two!' And they repeated. And repeated. And his bare feet trod on pieces of rock, then shells, then sand.

He turned and forced his hands under her armpits and hauled her high up the beach to where his jacket and boots waited for him as if they knew he'd be back. He rolled the girl onto her side and dropped heavily onto the sand beside her.

'Miss Eva! Can you hear me?' No answer. 'Miss Eva. There are dead bodies on the beach. Please don't look at them.'

The doctor's daughter uttered a weak groan and fell asleep.

CHAPTER TWENTY-NINE

Saturday 1 June
Tom

Water washed over Tom's feet and woke him.

Miss Eva?

He jolted up. The water was lapping at her feet too. It must be a higher than normal tide. He dragged her further up the beach. She did not respond, but she was breathing. He untied the remaining string on her the lifebelt and peeled it away – so decayed and frayed he wondered how it had kept her afloat. She did not stir at all. He recovered his wet jacket and spread it over her, hoping it would be a barrier against the wind.

In the sky, as though it were any other day, gulls laughed and circled and dived.

Blasts of air whipped through his damp shirt and trousers. He sat down on the sand, trembling, hugging his legs to hold in his warmth. What he saw, he could not understand. The chaos that riddled the shoreline and water was the material for a lifetime of nightmares. Yet, the impossible had happened for Miss Eva and himself. They were on dry ground.

He took deep breaths then stood and looked around the gorge. The harsh back end was heavily shadowed. It was rough scrub and walls of rock. Far above, at the top of the cliff, grass and straggly trees trimmed the rim. At the bottom of the rock wall that encircled the small beach, in the shadows beyond a straggle of low scrub, a sandstone overhang looked like it might offer protection from the wind.

Tom forced his legs to walk and winced when a broken shell dug into his foot. The rock walls around the gorge were like a fortress shutting them in. He examined the overhang and decided it would help protect them from the worst of the wind. He walked slowly down the sand and along the line of broken, lifeless bodies strewn on the beach. Some were knocking against wreckage in the water. None were the captain or any of the Carmichaels. He tried not to look but he knew each one by their clothes or build.

There were no survivors here. No crew. No passengers. No captain. No men rowing a lifeboat into the gorge. He lifted then dropped the soaked remains of a burlap wheat sack. No food.

Then he found a broken case that held the jagged remains of brandy bottles. He investigated with care and found two intact and full eight-ounce bottles and rinsed off the sodden wood shavings used for packing.

With a bottle in each hand he shuffled to another overhang. Deep in the cliff, like a twin to the cave he had already looked into, this overhang was partially hidden by patches of beaten bush. Tiny wrens flitted on the ground and in and out of the shrubs, nipping up invisible insects. They flew off when they saw him.

Tom placed his hand on the wall inside. It was wet and so was the ground. Water was filtering from the land above through the ancient rock.

He returned to the girl and turned back to stare at the land behind him.

'Damn it!' he yelled. They were trapped and their only way to escape was to swim into the sea, or to climb the towering wall up to the land above.

The young woman was all but dead to look at, but he watched and the jacket he had laid over her rose and fell faintly with her breath. Tom placed the brandy bottles in the sand beside her.

On his knees, he gently shook her shoulder. She was so cold.

'Miss Eva,' he said. 'We need to get to shelter.' He used the back of his icy fingers to touch her cheek. She stirred and her eyes opened into slits. Then she jerked and looked at him. She sat up suddenly and gazed at the scene left and right, the ocean, the bodies, the debris, then looked blankly at Tom.

'Mr Pearce!' Tom knew he could not protect her from everything that had happened and he watched and waited for her to remember.

'Oh! Oh no. No! Where is Mother? Father? The children?' Her voice came out thin and strained. Her hair was ragged strands streaking across her bruised face. Her mouth quivered and face crumbled. Tears welled then flooded her cheeks.

'I'm sorry, Miss Eva. I've not found anyone else yet,' Tom said. 'We're the only survivors on this beach but some might have reached beaches near here.' He rose slowly until he was on his feet again. 'We have to get out of the wind. I've found a shelter.' Tom's eyes pointed back at the overhang. 'Over there.'

He reached for her hand. She used her sleeve to wipe her face then let him raise her. He drew his damp jacket around her shoulders and supported her by her arm across the sand and over the scrubby grasses to the mouth of the gaping overhang. The floor was rough and covered in sand, rocks, weeds and blown-in twigs. And animal bones. But it was dry.

'Is it safe in here?' She asked, peering to see further in. Safe. What was safe? The ship had been safe with its lifeboats and strong crew.

Tom's foot scraped a space for her to sit, then he lowered her to the sand.

'I'll check around,' Tom said. The cave was shallow. The wind blew in, and out. It whistled through the rough ceiling and buffeted the back wall. No obvious danger. And no snakes as far as he could tell but it was winter and they'd be hidden and asleep.

Tom said to her, 'I have to leave you for a minute. You can watch me. I'm going to pick up something from where we were.'

She did not respond.

Tom's effort to walk to the shore was gargantuan. He collected the brandy bottles then gathered up his wet boots. He'd need them. But when he returned to the cave and saw how purple Eva's feet were, he slid his boots onto her feet instead.

She sat like a grey statue, staring out at the water and the cliffs and hearing the cracking of pieces of cargo as they smashed onto other cargo or half-submerged rocks. The sun had risen but its vague warmth would not fall into the cave. A few scudding clouds crept across the clear sky. Out in the gorge, light bounced off the rock walls and sharpened the white, yellow, orange and grey in the rocks that were so magical except for the tragedy their cousin beyond the gorge had conceived.

Far out beyond the narrow entrance to the gorge, the surf still pounded hard in and out, tumbling more scraps of wreckage onto the self-made reef across the gap.

'How could anyone get through that?' Miss Eva whispered.

'We survived,' Tom said quickly. 'You and me. And there were far stronger people on the *Loch Ard* than us.'

Their eyes met for a moment then Tom's moved away and rested on the brandy bottles. They were corked. But he had seen desperate crewmen in bunkrooms solve the problem of corks.

'I'm sorry Miss Eva. I'll need to borrow one of my boots for a moment.' He tried to smile at her, and thought he spotted a tiny glimmer of curiosity in her eye.

He put the bottle into the shoe and pounded the shoe on the cave wall, and soon the cork loosened. He repeated for the second bottle and a minute later returned the boot to her foot then handed her a bottle.

'Here, Miss Eva. Sip slowly. It'll warm you.'

She sipped, coughed, and sipped some more. Her cheeks turned pink. She pressed the bottle into the sand to rest it upright.

'You rescued our Margaret from the ocean,' she whispered. 'And now, Mr Pearce, you've rescued me.'

Tom said nothing. Despite what he'd said to her about other beaches and survivors, it could be that fifty souls had in the last few hours been lost to the ocean. He sipped the brandy and it burned. He did not care. A fire in the cave would be good but there was no striker to start one and he blinked the idea away.

'Mr Pearce … Tom,' Eva said. 'Please call me Eva.'

Tom nodded. He was exhausted, and hungry.

'Can I do anything for your head?' Eva asked.

'My head?'

'That's a bad cut.'

Tom touched his hand to his forehead and felt a sticky split and lump, but could not recall how or when it had happened. His knuckles were grazed from the rocks too, and his face from when he swam ashore the first time.

'It's nothing. I'll wash it in the sea later.'

Eva took two more sips of her brandy. Then, as though a plug had been pulled from a bath, she lay down again.

'I'll just rest a few minutes,' she muttered. And instantly she slipped deeply into sleep.

Tom covered her with his jacket, dragged a few branches of brush across the entrance to block some of the wind, hollowed out a patch of sand a few feet from her, and curled himself into it.

He woke, shivering. The wind had lessened, and the angle of sunlight hinted noon.

Eva slept on. Despite the bruises, her face was rested. Tom had never looked at her so intently because Mac had rules.

Mac. Gone too.

Tom turned his face to the ocean.

They were the only living humans in that walled gorge. If something did not change, it could be the last place either of them ever saw.

Hunger gripped his belly again. His throat was thick with a thirst that brandy could not quench. He trudged down to the shore and stepped tiredly along the sand again, checking the broken crates and scraps of furniture, hoping something edible might appear.

Half a dozen bodies swung on the tide a few feet out but he did not have the strength to pull them in, and he turned and let his eyes trace up around the cliffs that rose to the land above. The vertical rock walls seemed impassable. No path.

No easy line of greenery from the ground to the top that would give him enough footholds. But there must be a way.

Thirst drove him back to the other cave that he'd dismissed because of the damp. He touched the wet walls again and licked at a small patch. It was gritty and tasted of salt the wind had blown in. On his knees beside the wall where the sand was the wettest, he dug a hole and in a few minutes the hole half filled with silty water, which he lapped from his hands. The liquid coursed through his body. He dug the hole bigger and left it to fill while he returned to the other cave. Eva was still sound asleep.

He decanted some of his brandy into Eva's bottle until it was full. After another gulp of the remaining liquor, he poured the rest of it over his scraped knuckles and, with difficulty, over his forehead. It stung.

Back at the hole he filled the empty bottle with water then placed it with the brandy beside Eva. For the first time since he'd been on the *Loch Ard*, he slipped both hands into his trouser pockets. His right hand came out with Straz's green kerchief.

He could not remember how it got there but he sighed and shook his head at the loss of his friend.

Eva did not stir or move at all. To save her, he had to leave her.

'I'll be back as soon as I can,' he whispered.

CHAPTER THIRTY

Afternoon, Saturday 1 June
Tom

Shadows had begun to shade the western edge of the beach. It was early afternoon and precious daylight was wasting.

Rosellas screeched in the distant tops of the sheoaks in the high land above the caves.

Tom took time to measure with his eyes the arc of the gorge. He traced the wall that ran from the ocean to behind the caves and back to the ocean again, then wondered if a nearby beach had a direct way up to the land. He could try to swim around the rocks to find out, but a shudder went through him as he considered that ocean. He couldn't go back in. Not today.

The vertical sandstone walls behind the caves stared back at him. He glanced at the sea. The tremor of wreckage rose and fell with the water. No cries for help. No life except birds and fish.

It was time to go and he tried not to think how Eva would react if she woke before he returned. It surprised him that it was so easy, today, to call her Eva. On the ship, it would never have crossed his mind, but they were two people who had survived something that so many others had not and it placed them in a tiny world alone. For a moment, he wondered if he should take his boots from her, but the memory of her purple feet stopped him. He now wore only torn trousers and his course shirt. He studied the walls again letting his eyes travel several imaginary paths from the ground to the top and back down, then he took a breath and chose a starting point.

Three times he climbed a few yards up before slipping and tumbling back onto shrubbery and sand. After the third attempt, he stepped back to examine the wall above. He should have gone right not left from that last foothold.

He climbed again, searching for handholds and places for his bare toes to latch. It was entirely different to climbing rigging. He veered to his right along a ridge of stone; edged one hand up at a time and felt blindly for new handholds. Many minutes later, he misjudged his toe grip and both feet slipped, raining fragments of sandstone thirty feet towards the ground, and leaving him gripping a rock ledge with his fingertips and scrambling for somewhere to put his feet. The rock scraped all over his face and chest. His raw hands begged to let go. He shut his eyes and breathed deeply then eased up one knee. His toes felt their way and found a purchase point and slowly his foot took some of his weight. Then his other foot found a crevice.

He must be halfway. He climbed a few more feet then looked up. Far above, an eagle hovered on an air current. Tom shut his eyes and tried to ignore the pain in his arms and legs. When he looked, all the grip points were out of reach. The rock was quite smooth above him and it almost undid him when he had to wriggle down about ten feet, slide sideways to the left, then climb up from there. Thirst and hunger wracked his body. But the thought of Eva alone in the cave commanded him further.

Not far above him now, finches, and those fairy wrens again, were chirping to each other, fluttering about through the shrubbery on the land.

Then one of Tom's hands felt tree roots, and then the other felt soil and he fought the panic that made him want to rush this last bit. He took a deep breath and edged along until he found a small gap between the bushes then used his toes to thrust up until finally, blessedly, he dragged himself horizontally along his belly across sticks and grasses, and out of the gorge. He could smell real earth for the first time in months, and the subtle berry fragrance of fireweed.

But the sun was three quarters through the sky and there was no time to rest and smell things. He could not see into the caves, but nothing moved on the beach below except the horror at the waterline, and he prayed aloud that Eva would stay safe.

The trees made it hard to see which way to go and there were no clues. No smoke from a farmhouse, or sounds of people. So he turned east and angled slightly inland. He pushed through scratchy grasses and a few thorny shrubs for a short distance. A fly buzzed past his head. He waved it away and the motion of turning filled him with horror. He would never find the edge of that gorge again unless he marked it. He rushed back, peeling his shirt from his body. He ripped off a sleeve and tied it as high as he could on a sapling near where he had slithered from the gorge.

The land was almost flat but was covered with heath bush and clumps of sheoaks, and it was agony for his bare feet to walk through it. He set his shadow at two o'clock and walked.

Half an hour later, when Tom thought he might have covered barely a mile, a bird screeched above, and in the instant that he glanced up his foot caught on a mat of grasses and he crashed to the ground. He spat dirt from his mouth. He raised himself up on his forearms and saw that he had fallen across a faint trail less than a foot wide. And inches in front of his eyes were hoof marks from a shod horse. The prints were probably a day or two old, but they were enough. And they headed east.

The trail was easier under the tender skin on his feet and the faster progress lifted his spirits. Soon the trail merged with a wider, grassy cart-track that lacked recent wheel marks but the horse marks continued.

Another mile on, the trail drifted beside a thick stand of whispering sheoaks then over a soft ridge. As he passed the trees, he gazed far ahead, where the bushes were thinner and the ground became patches of meadow.

And there.

Two horsemen driving a flock of sheep away from him.

Tom halted. The sight jolted him and a trembling crashed over his body. The men were real and he had to find a way to stop them, immediately.

He hollered. He waved his hands above his head. He hollered again. The yell hurt his throat. The distance was too great and neither horseman responded. Tom fought his exhausted mind. The men would have the noise of the sheep, horses and perhaps dogs, about them, and they were probably calling to one another as well.

He stood on tip toes, shoved two fingers from each hand into the sides of his mouth and blew the loudest whistle of his life.

One of the horsemen stopped, put his hand on the rear of his saddle and turned his torso and head to look back.

CHAPTER THIRTY-ONE

Afternoon, Saturday 1 June
Eva

The wind murmured and dragged its fingertips in a dance over Eva's arms and neck and face. It crept across the cave walls behind her. She stirred and listened to it whine over holes in the rocks.

Then she remembered. She kept her eyes closed. She fought to shutter the horrors of her thoughts. She failed and gathered a picture of her family in her mind, determined to stay in this darkness with them.

In the end her bladder decided. She sat quickly. Tom was not there. In haste in case he was not far away, she staggered out and solved her need behind a bush next to the overhang's mouth then kicked sand over the humiliating patch.

The two brandy bottles stood at attention in the sand. They were full. She sniffed both then gulped down every drop of water and wondered where her rescuer had gone. And then she wondered too if her family had reached the beach.

Last night, her dress worn over her nightdress was heavy in the water, and now the two were too thin to keep her warm. Her feet flopped and rubbed on damp sand inside Tom's boots.

Small waves ran into the beach in a rush. They departed slowly. The roar and violence from the night had gone, as though the huge monster was napping.

She called out across the water. 'Tom!'

Nothing.

She turned and yelled into the rocky spaces behind her. 'Mr Pearce!' Only an echo of her voice answered.

She walked to the shoreline. Not far out in the water floated furniture, rope, a piece of piano, and sails. They crowded the shore, some stranded in the sand as the tide receded, some flushing out to return later or to be lost to the deep forever. A dead rooster too, and the steward's tray, she recognised, caked in sand.

There was an oval tin labelled Dr Lyon's Tooth Powders that skated in and out in an inch of water. Clothes tangled with each other. A broken crate of straw hats. A book of hymn music. There were even soggy, dissolving strips of dried fish and dried beef that until yesterday were stored carefully in salted barrels in the hold, but Eva guessed they would not be safe to eat. Fabrics that for the past three months were curtains, now snaked about in the shallows on their own strange courses. A walnut tobacco pipe too, and she recognised it but struggled to remember whose lower lip it had hung from. One of the older sailors?

There were the bodies amongst it all. Her eyes sprang from one to another. From a distance she examined them, detached. She could not feel their loss. None were her family. She looked at them as a doctor's daughter would. They were like rag dolls, tangled and artificial in the water. One almost naked, his clothes sucked off by the sea, and left ankle broken so severely that the foot fanned back and forth with the water. Two more bodies bobbed twenty feet from the shore. Two more close in.

Something deep in Eva's core became something she did not recognise. A horrible black grief began to cloak her, and it ran into every bone and muscle in her body.

'How can this be?' she whispered.

'How?' she shouted.

Tom's boots on her feet crunched in the sand.

A body lay face up in a foot of water just beyond a large crate.

The man, and she searched her memory, was Rancie – the carpenter.

His face rolled with the action of the water. She dared to lean in for a moment. His lips were black and swollen. His eyes bulged in sockets gawking at the sky, then the water rolled his head and the dead eyes looked blankly at her.

A long scream left her mouth. It blended with the gulls and the breeze. Then it was gone and she wondered if she had made any noise at all. Her heart pounded in her chest. Her feet thumped up the beach inside the boots. She ran clumsily towards a second cave. When she had almost reached it, she stopped as though she had run into a solid wall.

She whirled around. Looking. Out. Up. The cliffs. Like being stuck in a net. It was as though a huge chisel had chipped the walls from the land high above, and the sea had washed it all out until just the nameless isolated beach was left.

And where was Tom? Eva stood alone, dizzy and weak, with the day fading and with no food or water. A garbled moan echoed across the air. The walls towered high. They bounced the sound, hiding its source. A bird? An animal? Maybe the natives her father had told her about? Or was it Tom, injured? The moan rose again. Her breath came hard.

She had to hide. The caves would be too obvious and she cast her eyes about, searching for somewhere safe. On a rise of ground close to the rock face on her right was a patch of bush much denser than the others. She crouched low and stumbled to it and tucked in behind the bushes. Something rustled in the grasses near her and she forced herself to believe it was only lizards. She liked lizards.

An hour later, the light blue sky began to wash darker. It brought dusk and stinging cold air. And more sounds echoed across the gorge that she did not recognise. Finding Tom would have to wait until dawn.

'I should have brought his jacket,' Eva said angrily to herself. 'And the brandy.' It took a while to use her hands and a stick to scrape a saucer in the sand. Darkness fell fast and she curled her body inwards to keep the cold away.

Hunger kept her awake for a while. And the sound of the waves rolling in the gorge. But Eva slipped into jagged sleep and only stirred much later in the night when she heard the sounds of people.

CHAPTER THIRTY-TWO

Dusk, Saturday 1 June
Tom

The man trotted his horse towards Tom. When he was four yards away, he halted and stood in his stirrups. The knuckle of his forefinger inched the brim of his hat up his sweaty forehead.

'What you doing out here, mate?' The man looked Tom over and Tom remembered his cut face and sleeveless arm. 'And where's your boots?'

Tom could not find words. Everything. The fog. The shipwreck. The lost souls. Eva. It exploded as a new storm in his head and he could find no way to explain it.

'You drunk?'

The horse stepped around Tom, behind him. In front. Halted. Tom recalled he'd tipped brandy over his wounds. The man was sniffing the air as he circled.

In the distance, a dozen kangaroos loped south and vanished into scrub. The breeze, chilling and wintry, blew through Tom's clothes.

'No. No!' Tom said finally. His voice was hoarse. 'Shipwreck. Two miles back. The girl.' What was wrong with him? He could not even form a sentence.

'What? You playing a game?'

Then Tom's words lined up and he blurted them out.

'Last night, in the fog, our ship wrecked against cliffs. There's a girl. She needs help. Food. Water.'

The man on the horse was perhaps twenty-five and reminded Tom of another uncle he had not seen for years. Square jaw. Lanky body. Clear eyes.

The other rider trotted closer.

'So, who's this gloomy fellow?'

'Says there's a shipwreck, Wal.'

'There is!' Tom said. 'Please! Get help.'

Could it come to this … no one believing him while Eva was desperately stranded in that gorge?

'How many on board?' the first man asked.

'More than fifty. The *Loch Ard* from London.' And it seemed that the story finally became real to them. For a few seconds, they both froze.

'Damn hell!' the man named Wal yelled. 'You kidding?' His horse startled and turned a full circle on the spot.

'I've found a girl alive,' Tom said. 'There are bodies.' He bent and rested his hands on his knees. 'Do you have water?' he groaned.

The first man leapt down, unhitched his water bag from his saddle and passed it to Tom. 'Drink it slow. So, how many survivors all up?'

Tom stood upright and tried to resist gulping. He sipped at the water and it had a sweetness he had never known, and perhaps would never sense again.

'Only two. As far as I can tell.' He lowered the bag but did not hand it back. 'I'm Tom Pearce,' he said.

'Well Tom, I'm George, and this's Wally. The homestead we're at, it's barely a mile off. Come and get food and boots and we'll take you back to find the girl.'

Tom shook his head. 'I have to get back before dark. It's about two miles.' He pointed west. 'There's a blind gorge. A tall island's beyond it. I've put a rag – my sleeve – on a bush at the top of the gorge. The girl … Miss Eva. She … she must be freezing by now. Please bring blankets. And food.'

George stood in his stirrups again and his eyes traced the distant coast. 'I reckon I know the gorge you mean,' he said. 'We'll need ropes too.' Then he rummaged in his saddle bag. He handed Tom a cloth bag.

'Bit of bread left in there and some dried beef. Take the water bag with you. And Tom Pearce … we'll bring help as soon as we can.' He looked at the other man. 'Wally, I'll ride to Glenample fast and get help. You and the dogs can keep the sheep moving back.'

CHAPTER THIRTY-THREE

Dusk, Saturday 1 June
Tom

Tom nibbled at a little of the bread and beef as he struggled back along the cart track, but soon he scrunched the bag closed.

Terrified that the light would be gone before he reached the gorge, he moved as fast as he could. Then he froze. Something was wrong. He did not recognise where he was.

He had missed the narrow horse track that he'd tripped into earlier. He backtracked and felt ill when he found it.

For barely a minute, he closed his eyes and listened to the chatter in nearby treetops – the sound of parrots screeching the end of the day. When he felt focussed enough he scrambled on again. Soon the track melted into scrub and he pushed his way through scratchy bush and over sticks and stones that dug into the soles of his feet.

His body had begun to shake. It was a perilous sign of fatigue and he doubted his strength would last much longer. His throat hurt and he could not think of an inch of his body that was not aching. His head ached too and it was the thing that nearly finished him.

But he could hear the sea now. The growing thunder of the ocean steered him towards it. As the last strand of sunlight speared between western trees, it washed onto the sleeve he had left as a marker at the brink of the gorge.

Below in the darkness, nothing moved except the charcoal shapes of cargo laying in a black fringe along the waterline, and the black dots of wreckage and other losses that rose and fell in the sea.

Tom dropped the empty water bag on the ground. He removed his shirt. The iciness of winter smacked his bare skin. Quickly, he tied the remains of his shirt into a sling for the food and slung it across his back.

He opened his mouth to yell down to tell Eva that he was there, but he shut it fast. A voice yelling out in the dark could terrify her. As the last glow from the setting sun brushed gold across the tops of treetops in the west, he found a firm shrub for a handhold and lowered himself over the edge. The sandstone scraped at his knees, his torn toes, his shins, his belly, his chest, and even his armpits; and the thought came to him that he could never have climbed the wall wearing boots anyway. His bare toes and fingers were all that held him to the impossible cliff and he wondered if he should have waited for the men with ropes.

As soon as he was below the gorge's rim, it was night. In his mind, he tried to read the cliff. When the ship had gone down, he had battled the violent ocean. Now, from somewhere within himself he fell into another level of awareness – an exhausted kind of consciousness. He imagined himself blind, and closed his eyes.

His toes felt for and found a crevice. Then a piece of root. Then another crevice. His fingers followed; felt for grips. Found grooves, then more tiny spaces. His eyes stayed shut. His nose stayed so close to the wall that it scraped several times. He got stuck but repeated what he'd done that afternoon, reversing track, and changing direction. Feeling his way.

The wind swirled in the gorge, slapping at the cliff face and buffeting Tom's ears.

A small ledge broke away under his feet and the crumbs of stone chuckled down the wall beneath him, but his fingers held firm. His heart pounded so hard he was certain it would shove him away from the wall but he hung on and crept sideways.

Another ledge, another crevice. Then something tapped the back of his leg and he felt ill. What terror was this attacking him now? He eased to the left and something else touched his bare back. He risked a hand to feel for his attacker and found leaves. On a bush. On the ground.

The cold sand beneath his feet was paradise. Then he was rushing blindly, falling, running between the shrubs to the entrance of the overhang where he'd left Eva. He yelled into the darkness and his voice, far weaker and crustier than he had ever heard it, echoed out to him. He dropped the sling of food and crawled into the blackness, feeling along the sand. His jacket. The bottle of brandy. The empty bottle of water. No one.

He pulled his jacket on then sat, exhausted, and sipped three mouthfuls of brandy, which burned and warmed him. Where was she?

'Miss Eva!' he called out, but his voice was becoming worse every time he used it. 'Eva!' He shuffled exhausted over the sand. Starlight began to illuminate shapes against white beach. No bodies that he could see – perhaps taken out on the high water. Eva was not in the other cave.

She was gone.

Down on the shoreline, he dragged his shredded feet through the water, soaking the tattered hems of his trousers. Cold salt water stung his feet, and soothed them and he ran his hands through it too and splashed some on his face. He wondered if perhaps Eva had done the same? Had madness and grief overtaken her? Had she walked into the sea, perhaps to swim to find her family?

Why did he leave her? She probably thought he'd abandoned her. He should have written a message to her in the sand in the cave.

So much wreckage was knocking about in the shallows. He stood there for longer than he wanted, then dragged himself back towards the cave entrance.

A male voice came from up high. 'Hello!'

Far up, where he had left his sleeve, a yellow light moved from side to side. For a moment, Tom was overwhelmed and a sob gulped up from his chest and out of his throat.

Finally, he was not alone. Someone else could take charge of this hell. They would find Eva.

'Hello! Are you there, Tom Pearce?' Most of the words weakened in the wind but he heard them.

'Yes! Yes!' he yelled. He could not tell if his voice had carried. Then he whistled four, five, six times, losing power with each effort.

'Please come. Please find us,' he begged the air, and he dropped to his knees in the sand and wept.

CHAPTER THIRTY-FOUR

Evening, Saturday 1 June
Tom

The voices echoed. Tom sat, shivering. A lantern began to descend the cliff like a bead of honey on a string, far faster than Tom had come down. Then another lantern followed.

When the first reached the ground, Tom whistled again, then called out until someone ran and knelt beside him.

'You're a bloody miracle, mate,' George said. His face was gold in his lantern light. 'How the heck did you get down that rock without rope?' He had a tin bucket that he stood in the sand.

Tom shook his head. 'I can't find her,' he said. Then grief heaved inside him and he did not care that he was weeping again. Too much had happened. Too many lost.

'I can't find her! I don't know … maybe she walked into the sea.' A thought leapt at him that a boat may have come and rescued her and his eyes widened. 'Or maybe someone else found her!'

'Tom. Settle down,' George said. He gripped Tom on the shoulder. 'If she's anywhere here, we'll find her. But let's wait till Mr Gibson's down.'

Tom looked into the cave at the soft shadows falling on the rock and sand. A man strode up – tall, lean, with a tight beard – carrying a bag and another lantern.

'Tom, this is Hugh Gibson, my boss,' George said.

Tom stood and Gibson shook his hand. He looked at Tom with a question in his face. And doubt.

'Hello Tom.' Gibson glanced across at George.

'Tom says the girl's gone missing,' George said.

Gibson's manner hinted at frustration. His eyes floated around the cave and narrowed when they stopped at the brandy bottles in the sand.

'A shipwreck?' he said, ignoring George's comment about Eva. 'Let's see.' Scottish accent. Diluted by a decade or two perhaps.

Tom and George followed Gibson towards the shore but they had barely walked twenty paces when Gibson's manner shifted. He stopped solid. His shoulders froze. He held his lantern out in front then strode along the tideline a few more yards. Two bodies tumbled in the water beyond him.

He turned. 'How many on board?'

'More than fifty, sir. The *Loch Ard* from London.'

'My God,' Gibson muttered. 'Where's the ship?'

'Gone.' Tom pointed into the wind. 'Broke up on a ledge beyond those cliffs.' He grabbed Gibson's sleeve. 'Sir, please help me find Miss Eva! She's a passenger about my age. Her father was the doctor on board. But she's lost! She was asleep in the cave when I left to find help, but she's missing now.'

He felt the world slip away and his face smacked on grit and shells. When he woke he was lying on dry sand under a blanket. The way the wind blew around him told him he was inside the cave where he'd left Eva. He opened his eyes.

'Mr Gibson?' he yelled, sitting fast. 'George?'

He listened. Nothing.

Then, a faint yell. 'She's over here!'

Tom flung the blanket aside and nearly fell over the socks and boots that had appeared on his feet. He staggered out towards the light. Mr Gibson, barefoot, was holding a lantern while George stumbled towards him with Eva draped limp across his arms. Tom gasped. At the cave, he cast the blanket flat and George lowered Eva onto it and they wrapped each side of the blanket over her.

Tom put his head close to hers. 'Eva?'

'Tom, let me,' Gibson said gently. His fingers brushed a tangle of Eva's hair from her face. He put his ear close to her mouth. 'She's breathing, but very weak.' He took his coat off and laid it over her.

'We have to warm her, sir,' George said. 'I'll light a fire.'

'No, I'll light it. You ride back to Glenample and get men – everyone possible. We'll need more rope. Oil for the lanterns. Whatever else that's quick to bring. And tell my wife what's happened. She'll know what to do.' He turned towards the sea as if to hope that there might be others to be rescued by then too. 'And the buggy,' he added softly when he looked down at Eva.

Gibson glanced back towards the impossible rock wall.

'I'll come and help you get started on the rope,' he said to George. 'Take a lantern up and leave it at the top so you can find us again.'

Tom sat on the cold sand. Eva was so white and so still beside him that she seemed barely alive. Gibson returned with sticks and a piece of a bookcase, and lit a fire.

'George brought coffee and food,' he said. He pulled a billy can from the bucket and slowly the coffee heated beside the flames. Its scent forced Tom to close his eyes. It was as though he was back on the ship.

'What's this?' Gibson sniffed the brandy bottle, then sloshed some into the billy. They took turns sipping hot coffee from the single mug. Gibson pulled fresh bread and cool cheese from a rectangular tin and it was the best food Tom had ever eaten.

'How will we get her up there?' Tom asked, his eyes pointing at the darkness.

'We'll need a sling of some sort,' Gibson said.

Tom put his hand on Eva's cheek, and it felt a little warmer than before. He grabbed the lantern and he and Gibson walked the shoreline again. A piece of sail was on the beach but it was half-buried in the sand and tangled in a mass of broken spar and weed. Another piece of sail was in the water, coming and going on the waves.

'I'll get it,' Gibson said. He waded out and dragged the wet sail onto the beach – the remains of one of the bowsprit's triangular jibs. It'd do. Tom found five or six yards of rope.

Back in the cave, Gibson watched as Tom teased tangles from the rope.

'You were a passenger Tom, or a sailor?'

'Apprentice midshipman, Mr Gibson. Do you have a knife?' He took a folding knife from Gibson. Brass handled and a good weight and it was sharp enough to cut the rope into four pieces.

Tom shut out the world and focussed on doing something instinctive. He took his time and knotted a rope to each corner of the sail. The fourth piece he spliced into an eye then secured the three lengths onto it.

'Brilliant,' Gibson whispered. 'Tom, what happened?'

It took Tom a second to realise Gibson meant the wreck.

'The fog. The reckoning said we were much further out.' Then Tom remembered the smell and that he should have realised how close they were to land. A sick hollowness swallowed him. He could have stopped it all.

Eva moaned and began to move and Tom crabbed madly over the sand to her.

'Miss Eva. Eva! It's Tom. People are helping us now. We're safe.'

Eva's eyes opened. Closed. Blinked. She raised her head and looked at the lantern. At Gibson. At Tom. Then she tried to sit and Tom helped her.

'Eva, this is Mr Gibson,' Tom said. 'He's come to help us get to safety.'

Eva studied Gibson. Then her eyes traced Tom from toe to head.

'Tom,' she said. 'We have to fix your wounds.'

Gibson laughed aloud and Eva flinched.

'I can't believe it! You two are the toughest folk I've ever met.'

For a second, Eva smiled.

Then she asked, 'Did you find anyone else?'

Tom shook his head. Eva's eyes closed and she drew in a long breath. She looked back at him and sighed. Gibson offered her the coffee cup and she gulped from it then devoured the rest of the cheese and bread. Her first food since the final dinner in the cuddy the night before.

A little over an hour later, voices called from the distance. 'Mr Gibson!'

CHAPTER THIRTY-FIVE

Late at night, Saturday 1 June
Eva

Eva wore Gibson's coat and waited at the bottom of the cliff.

The sleep and food had helped her body but her mind had begun a numb swirl of panic. Where was her family? Were they together somewhere waiting to be rescued and thinking it was her who had been lost? She could barely breathe as her thoughts became a storm.

But the cold wind and the activity of the men snapped her back to that square foot of sand she stood on. She hugged the coat close and tried to remember Gibson's instructions. He'd said something about them using this sling Tom had made to help her up the cliff. Men's voices shouted down and somewhere up there a horse whinnied into the night.

'Do you understand, Miss?' Gibson asked her.

She nodded. 'I know it's the only way out, Mr Gibson. And, if there's truly no one else on this beach, I don't want to be here a minute longer than I must.'

Gibson looked at her closely, then turned his eyes to the cliff.

'You really are a tough one, Miss Eva. I doubt my wife would have got through this. And that boy. What's he made of? Iron? He survived the wreck, pulled you from the surf, then climbed out of this gorge, and back down. Without rope.'

'Hoy, sir!' someone called from above. 'Ready up here!'

'Are you ready, Miss?'

'Thank you, Mr Gibson,' Eva said. She leaned on his offered arm. The sling lowered into view and Tom crawled out of it onto the sand.

'Just testing it,' he said to Eva's unasked question.

The lanterns lit up two ropes dangling down the cliff. The limp sail waited at the bottom of one. The other had a large loop.

'This man, William, is going to ride up next to you,' Tom said. 'Are you ready, Eva?' All eyes were on her and for a silly moment Eva was aware of her matted hair and ripped clothes. The canvas was on the ground and she sat in the middle of it and gripped two of the ropes.

'I'm ready.'

'I'll be right up after you,' Tom said.

A man stepped into the rope loop beside her.

'Right-o!' he called to the surface above. He whistled.

'Are the men up there strong enough?' Eva asked him.

'They're using the horses to pull us up, Miss,' William said. 'Hang on tight.'

Despite some harsh bumping against the rock wall, the ascent took minutes. When she reached the top, lanterns illuminated a rig of wood and improvised pulleys and soon Eva was standing looking out at the dark ocean and hearing a coastline of surf. William moved her away from the edge and stayed with her. Men jostled around in the dark holding the harnesses of several horses. They lowered the sling for Tom, then individually pulled up Gibson and the last of his men. Lantern-light glowed on relieved faces.

Men were mounting their horses.

'Where's the buggy?' Gibson asked.

'Just a stone's throw,' someone answered.

The wind gusted in from the sea.

'George,' Gibson called.

'Yes, Mr Gibson!' George answered in the dark. He approached.

'We need to let the police know as fast as we can. There'll be wreckers here looting the moment word gets out.'

'I'll ride over to Port Campbell,' George said. 'The *Loch Ard* from London?' he asked Tom.

Tom nodded.

It was after midnight. No moon. The stars sprinkled cool light that separated dark trees from shrubs.

'Right,' Gibson answered. 'Get Swale to telegram the Harbour Master in Melbourne. They'll have to send men to guard the cargo, and whatever's left of the ship …'

The silence added: *And collect the bodies.*

CHAPTER THIRTY-SIX

Sunday 2 June
Tom

The night snapped cold air at everything. It smelled of salt and trees and earth. On the plank seat in front of Tom and Eva, the dark shape of a boy sat hunched. The boy's collar was up, and he was driving the horse that pulled the buggy.

Eva had fallen sound asleep with her head slumped against Tom's arm. He tugged her blanket back up over her shoulder then shifted further down into his own and a sliver of warmth radiated through the blankets from her body. Tom's determination to stay awake until they were safely at the homestead failed and he woke groggily as the buggy clattered into a yard. The silhouette of a shawled woman ran from the house towards them.

'Oh my. Oh my!' she said.

Another woman followed close behind her.

Eva startled awake and cried out.

The first woman leaned in. 'Don't be afraid. I'm Lavinia,' she told them. For Tom it was like she was talking under water. He tried to shake the dead sleep from his head. The woman put a hand briefly on his, but they were there to help Eva. One on each side, they eased her to the ground. Eva glanced back at Tom. He nodded at her.

'We're safe now,' he said. He watched her go.

The women crossed their arms behind Eva's back, and walked her into the house. Shadows passed across dimly lit windows.

'You right mate?' Wally grabbed one of Tom's arms and eased him down.

'Thanks,' Tom said. The house was ten steps away. Six. Two.

There was the dull thud of horses at a gallop, then at a trot. Circling in the yard. Boots landing on gravel. Men calling orders.

The buggy's wheels crackled on stones. Stable doors squeaked open.

Gibson, still bootless, came up beside Tom.

'Let's get you to the kitchen, Tom. Food, then a bed.'

'Thanks,' Tom whispered again. The light from lamps inside made him blink. Gibson led him through a small drawing room to the kitchen where one of the women who'd helped Eva from the buggy stood ladling something at the stove. Eva was not there. Gibson pressed Tom onto a chair at the table.

'Tom, this is Eliza, our cook.'

The woman smiled tiredly. She placed a bowl of chunky glistening soup in front of Tom.

'Where's Eva?' Gibson asked Eliza.

'Poor girl said she was too tired to eat,' Eliza said. 'Mrs Gibson's walked her to bed. Would you like some soup, Mr Gibson?'

Gibson nodded. 'The men will appreciate some as well.'

'Yes, sir,' she said.

The hot soup warmed Tom. Soft vegetables in a salty stock.

'Mr Gibson,' he said. 'Can you get word out to look for the others?'

Their eyes connected. Gibson sat and his face said what Tom was thinking. It was unlikely there would be others.

'The Port Campbell police will take care of it, and they'll send word to the harbour authorities. But I know this coast, Tom, and it's a vile one. Mostly rock, and only a couple of beaches near where you and Miss Eva came in. I doubt we'll find many.'

In bustled his wife. She stopped and Tom tried to stand.

'No, no! You sit. Finish your soup. Then Hugh'll show you where you can wash, and sleep. Actually,' and she stood back and put her hands on her hips. 'You're badly cut. Your hands and head. I'll clean them up. Good grief! How did you not break a bone?'

'His feet too,' Gibson said. 'When he gives me my boots back.' He grinned. 'Lavinia dear, this is Tom Pearce.'

Tom tried to smile. 'Good evening, ma'am,' he said. 'They're just scratches.'

Mrs Gibson shook her head. She pulled a round tin from a cupboard. 'That girl's already asleep. And the bruises on her – my goodness.'

Tom felt their eyes on him while he finished the soup then Mrs Gibson dipped squares of gauze in salt water to wash dried blood and dirt from the cuts on his face, hands and feet.

'Mr Gibson,' Tom said. 'The bed sounds good.'

Gibson led Tom from the kitchen.

Tom did not remember another thing until he woke the next morning to the soft warble-song of magpies. A sliver of grey sky peeped past a curtain.

A currawong called. Then Tom heard a wail.

A heavy quilt was over him. He flung it back and leapt out of bed. He looked down. On his legs were someone else's long flannel under-drawers that bunched beyond his ankles and over his feet. On his top half was a linen shirt he did not recognise. He could not remember at all removing his clothes or putting those things on.

Another sob. No other clothes were in the room, but a course towel hung from on a hook behind the door and he snatched it down. He tugged it about his waist, gathered it in a fist at his navel, opened the door and rushed to the kitchen doorway, skidding on the under-drawers that dragged around his feet. For a moment, the smell of baking bread clouded his thoughts.

'Tom!' Eva leapt from a chair and threw her arms around his neck. Her reaction surprised him. Not an action any proper woman would ever do, and Mrs Gibson, standing back beyond the table, looked startled. But then, to Tom it became one of the most natural things that could happen that morning. Then Eva seemed to remember herself and released him. She retreated a couple of steps. A bandage was around the palm of her right hand.

'Tom, I'm so glad to see you.' A black ribbon drifted from behind her head onto her left shoulder. She was wearing a dark-blue dress slightly too big. The toes of soft, brown slippers poked from below the hem. Strained grey creases underlined her red and glistening eyes. She glanced down at his towel and redness flushed her cheeks.

Tom remembered his under-drawers and their fisted covering.

'I'm sorry. I couldn't find my clothes.'

Mrs Gibson spoke. 'Apart from your jacket, your clothes are ruined Tom but we've washed them in case they're important to you, and they'll be dry soon. My housekeeper Alice is hunting out something for you to wear.'

'Thank you, ma'am. The only thing I'd want from my clothes if it's still there … there was a green kerchief in a pocket.'

Mrs Gibson looked like she wanted to ask something, but she didn't.

'We have it. I'll get it back to you when it's dry. And Tom, Eva's been telling me about how you pulled her from the sea.' She softened her voice. 'Can I ask your age?'

'I'm nearly nineteen, Mrs Gibson.'

'Such courage for someone so young,' she whispered.

And then it struck Tom again, like a brick in the face, that he should now be on the *Loch Ard*, which yesterday should have tied up to a pier in Hobsons Bay. He was not unloading cargo. He was not watching Gibb spend a few minutes with each passenger, shaking hands and sharing stories, as they disembarked to the pier and off into Melbourne. Mac was not there signing forms for the Customs Officers, or making sure each crewman had the correct shore leave allotted to use after they'd emptied the ship of her cargo.

And Eva. She was not with her family settling into a Melbourne hotel.

What now?

Mrs Gibson interrupted his thoughts. 'It'll be in all the newspapers over the next day or so. They'll call you a hero, Tom.'

There was no joy in her voice.

The thought made Tom feel ill. He had barely pulled one person from the ocean.

'I'm sorry ma'am, but I hope not. I hope others have survived and that there are more stories of saved lives. I'm not a hero.'

Eva lowered herself to the chair. Her movements were slow. Heavy. She turned over the floral handkerchief in her battered hands.

'Hugh's taken some men to meet with Constable Graham,' Mrs Gibson said, 'to keep looters from the gorge.

There's some legal process that's to happen, to do with all the insurance and ownership business.'

'I'd like to go out with them, Mrs Gibson, if I can. To help find survivors, or if they need to identify … anything.'

'Yes, of course,' Mrs Gibson said. A woman entered carrying folded trousers, shirt and waistcoat in a neat pile. 'Tom this is Alice, and some clothes for you. After you've eaten, I'll call one of the men to take you to the gorge. Do you ride?'

Tom had rarely ridden a horse, and not for years.

'A little ma'am.' Most of his body ached. How much worse could it get?

'Your jacket is still drying so I'll find you one of Hugh's, and a hat.'

The sound of hooves on gravel made them all turn their heads. Tom glanced at Eva. Her eyes had lit up.

CHAPTER THIRTY-SEVEN

Sunday 2 June
Eva

Inside Eva, hope chilled. Gibson scraped his boots on a mat and came in the rear kitchen door.

He stood near the end of the table. His hat swept against his trouser leg and his other hand flapped a fly from his face. Eva glanced at Tom who stood there in bare feet, long underdrawers and a clenched towel.

Gibson shook his head gently and a painful emptiness rose inside Eva.

'No one, yet. I'm sorry,' he said. He let his words settle. Eva could feel everyone's eyes on her. 'The tide has taken out all the dead again, and some of the floating cargo.'

'Can we get more help?' Tom asked.

'It's coming. George got to Port Campbell around dawn,' Gibson said. 'The police sent a telegram to Melbourne and George waited there until they got the reply.'

'He must be exhausted,' Lavinia said. 'Like the rest of you.'

'We're alright,' Gibson said, a little gruffly, not looking at her. 'A bunch of officers from Colac are on their way to protect the wreckage. And men are coming from the shipping company in Melbourne. I'm sorry Miss Eva, and Tom, but word is out about the wreck. Two of my men were going after a boomah and spotted a couple of scroungers on the track from Warrnambool. They had a horse pulling an empty hay cart.' He nodded at Lavinia who was holding a teapot. She poured steaming tea into a mug.

Eva had to ask. 'I'm sorry. What's a "scrounger"? And a "boomah"?'

Tom laughed and Eva felt heat flush her face. But his smile was kind.

'Australian slang,' Tom said. 'A scrounger's a wretch who steals from a tragedy, like a train accident …'

'Or a shipwreck,' Eva said.

'Yes. And a boomah's a big kangaroo. Farmers hunt them for meat and skins.'

'Meat?' Eva asked.

'For themselves and their dogs. It's good meat for the cost of a bullet.'

'Anyway,' Gibson said, 'they turned back after they were challenged, but I wager they'll not go far. I've left a couple of men watching the gorge until the police get there.'

'I'll ride out when you go,' Tom said. Eva felt like a part of herself was leaving. This sailor who until a day ago had been almost a stranger now felt like a link to everything she had ever known. She wanted to ask him to stay. Except … he might find a Carmichael.

'You'd be welcome if you're up to it,' Gibson said. He looked at Tom's towel. 'Once you've dressed. Also, the police would like you both to help with a list of every person on board to cross check with the list when it comes from London. They need it as soon as possible. We should probably do it now so it's done.'

Gibson pulled out a pocket notebook and pencil while Tom listed the crew starting with the captain and ending with the stowaway. Eva told the names of her family, hardly believing that they may all be gone. She listed the other passengers too, then, suddenly, it hit her and she slapped her hand to her chest.

'Oh my goodness! My brother, William. He's a sailor but I believe he's working at the docks in Melbourne! Could we get a message to him to tell him I'm here?'

Lavinia Gibson fled the kitchen. A drawer opened in the next room, then shut, and she returned with a letter folder, and pen and ink.

'We'll do it immediately,' she said.

'Miss,' Mr Gibson said to Eva, folding the list into his pocket. 'I'm sorry I don't have better news. If all goes well, we should find some survivors today.'

Eva took a breath. 'I hope they're all safe somewhere.' A sharp desire to change the subject rose in her belly. 'But tell me,' she asked as brightly as she could summon, 'what are the … scroungers … looking for?'

'Oh, valuable things. Silver and glassware from the first-class galley. Liquor barrels. Undamaged cargo. Cash and jewellery that passengers may have brought.' He stopped to sip his tea. 'The port authority has warned that the *Loch Ard*'s manifest listed thousands of gallons of brandy and wines. Thieves know what to look for. Most cargo is probably sunk, but some of the professional wreckers actually take men and equipment to dive the wreck.'

The blood washed from Eva's face and she felt faint. The thought of anyone, even thieves, going into that water of death made her ill.

CHAPTER THIRTY-EIGHT

Sunday 2 June
Tom

Tom waited in the dusty yard dreading what he was about to do – return to the gorge.

The Gibson's sandstone house stood behind him. In front of him, quarters for the workers bounded the western side of the large work yard, and sturdy sheds and stables dotted the southern edge.

The boy, who Gibson had said was called Jack, was preparing two horses at the stables and Tom walked over to him.

'Hello Jack.'

'Mr Tom, morning,' Jack said with forced politeness.

'I've just realised this farm must run close to the ocean. I can smell the salt.'

'About a half mile as the bird flies,' Jack said. He stood back from the stirrup and measured it with his eyes. He looked fourteen, if that. Straw-haired with an already leathered-faced, like a saddlebag. 'If you'd wrecked a bit more east,' Jack added, 't'wards Melbourne, lots more of ya might've got saved. More beaches further east.'

The answer was harsh but not cruel. And Tom wished they'd got a bit more east … all the way to Melbourne.

The door of the house closed and Hugh Gibson paced towards them.

'Sorry, Jack,' Tom said. 'I'm not much of a rider. Could you help me up?'

Tom's horse followed Gibson's and the saddle soon found two of Tom's backside bones that were rarely challenged on a ship.

The sun shone between clouds that swept from the southeast. The wind cut through their clothes, and the air was colder than the day before. They dismounted near the cliff, spun their reins over branches and crunched through the scrub, listening as the ocean rumbled below, to the place where Tom had visited twice the evening before.

Wally was there and Tom noticed that the men had built a sort of davit to raise things from the beach more easily. The sling had already been used a few times that morning and some books were laid out on it, drying. They were water damaged but may be readable once dry. None were the captain's log. On the branch nearby, Tom's tattered shirt sleeve was still there, tangled into the bush now.

'Mr Gibson,' Wally said. 'Tide's brought in two bodies since you left.' His eyes flicked to Tom's for a moment then down to the beach.

Far below, a couple of Gibson's men were dragging whatever cargo they could to above the high-water line to prevent more being sucked out on the ebb tide. Crates, barrels, timber wreckage, and random scraps of blankets and sail were strewn about like seaweed after a storm.

'Where are they?' Gibson asked. 'The bodies.'

'They've wrapped them in some sail and put them in that cave. Two women.'

Now both men looked at Tom.

'There were only four women,' Tom said. 'And two little girls.'

One of those four women was sitting in a homestead a couple of miles away, which meant at least one body in the cave would be a Carmichael.

Gibson frowned at Tom. 'You sure you're up for another visit down there?'

He wasn't. 'I am,' Tom said.

Tom named the bodies. Eva's older sister, and Eva's mother. Cold and lifeless.

In the cave, someone handed Gibson a piece of folded cloth and inside it lay a gold watch.

'Slipped out of the older lady's pocket when we carried her up the beach,' the man said.

'Mr Gibson!' one of the men yelled from the waterline. 'Another body!'

A man was wading into the water, slinging a rope out as far as he could. Tom and Gibson ran to the waterline. Finally the rope landed over an ankle and the man pulled the body to the shore.

'It's Reginald Jones,' Tom said quietly. Jones was not wearing any sort of lifebelt and looked a lot like he'd been smashed against rocks before he'd died.

Tom and Gibson spent another half hour scanning the water but it was clear no more bodies were coming in on the tide.

Tom didn't like being there.

'Mr Gibson, can we go back up, and maybe ride further around the cliffs?'

At the top, he hauled himself onto his horse. His body trembled. He'd seen dead bodies before, but today had been different.

To the west, the ground rose slowly through light bush. Gibson rode ahead and in minutes they were at the rim of another gorge. Beyond it was the island that had peeled the *Loch Ard* apart. The sheer rock walls a few feet ahead of their horses' hooves did not drop to a soft beach like the one Tom and Eva had crawled onto, but fell into a pit of deep, violent water that smashed hard under a harsh overhang. No beach. No survivors. Just more debris smashing about.

Further ahead they heard yells and Tom's backside bones were grateful when Gibson dismounted and suggested they walk.

Three men, one whom Tom recognised from the night before, were easing a rope out through a pulley and stock. Tom did not trust his head or legs for balance. He crawled to the edge. In the sea, a long way down from where he looked, a bloated body bobbed in the ocean. One of Gibson's men hung on a rope at the bottom of the cliff, trying to catch it. An impossible task. When dirt and rocks crumbled over the edge, Gibson called to abandon the attempt.

'Do you recognise him, Tom?' Gibson asked.

Black trousers. Light shirt. No beard. He could be any of a dozen men. Too far away to even guess his build but he was not Captain Gibb or Mac.

'A crewman,' Tom said sadly, thinking of his bunkmates, and Straz. 'I'm not sure which one.'

Tom and Gibson rode back to Glenample with the sun behind them. Eva was sat tensely in an armchair in the drawing room. Mrs Gibson was perched opposite on a small, plain couch, sewing buttons on a shirt.

The hope in Eva's eyes stabbed at Tom's heart. He crouched in front of her and saw her colour wash away. And he saw that she knew it would be bad news.

'Eva. I'm sorry. They've found no survivors yet.' He paused. She waited. 'But they recovered some dead.'

Tom knew this moment – this place of "hearing" – himself. It existed somewhere between the sheltered, elevated part of your mind when you believed, even hoped, someone was alive, and that abyss you fell into as you learned they were forever gone. A few syllables were all that separated those two places.

Eva's life would never be the same.

'They found Reginald Jones's body,' Tom said.

Eva pressed her fingers over her mouth. 'He was with me,' she said. 'He swam off with Art Mitchell.'

Tom inhaled for strength. He looked at her.

'I'm sorry, Eva,' he said, 'but your mother's body, and your older sister's too.' He did not say how torn the bodies were, shredded on rocks, pecked by gulls.

The room was silent for a few seconds. Mrs Gibson quietly put her sewing aside.

Eva closed her eyes, then opened them. They were wet but she did not weep. She inhaled, long. Slow.

'Did they have lifebelts on?' she asked. 'My father was trying to get Mother's on her when Raby and I left them.'

'They both did. I guess that's why they …' then he regretted starting the sentence. 'Why they floated.'

He held out the small bundle wrapped in cloth and she took it into her hands.

'We found this,' Tom said.

Eva lay it on her lap and unfolded the cloth.

'My father's watch,' she whispered.

'Your mother had it. It slipped out of her clothing as they were bringing her in.' Tom stopped talking.

No one spoke. Eva traced the rim of the watch with a finger then gently rewrapped it in the cloth.

'And no one else?' Mrs Gibson asked.

'No ma'am.'

There would be reasons – sharks, undertow, people trapped inside the ship. Not things Tom would mention.

Only the sea and the heavens would hold the individual memories.

CHAPTER THIRTY-NINE

Tuesday 4 June
Glenample
Eva

For Eva, the following days became a blend of whispered conversations in other rooms and the arrival of several reporters from Victorian newspapers. Men came from the shipping company too, and a bush chaplain named Mr McIntyre.

Lavinia made sure the visitors were all well fed and she arranged for their muddy travelling clothes to be dried in front of the kitchen stove and brushed clean. She had the shearers' hut scrubbed out, and she borrowed extra bedding from a nearby farm.

She shepherded Eva too, and insisted that each official or reporter asked her permission to interview either survivor.

And whenever Eva sat opposite a reporter, Eva made sure she buried her grief. It was her own decision. She'd read enough newspapers to know the sort of wording they'd come up with. The woman "was suffering from fits of hysteria" or "was senseless with grief". If they saw her in the small night hours, it would be true, but something deep inside drove Eva's desire to honour her lost.

On the third or fourth day, a reporter rode in with a camera and took photos of Tom and Eva, then galloped away again.

Hugh Gibson became more tired each day, and Eva heard Lavinia say to a reporter she had never seen him this exhausted and that the only thing keeping him moving was that, even though less likely each day, his men or the police may find more survivors.

On Tuesday after lunch, Eva insisted she would be fine to walk by herself for an hour. She wore a thick coat but left it open. The cold whipping through her clothes reminded her that she was alive. It whipped across her face too and blew cold tears back towards her ears. She let it. Being alone meant she could release a measure of the pain.

Apart from William whom she had not heard from yet, her whole family had vanished in an instant. Not just her family either, but also their plans. Their future. Nothing would be the same. Eva had made sure that the clothes she had worn in the sea were kept. For her they were a strange link to her real self. She also had her father's watch and the three rings taken from her mother's fingers, which she kept on her nightstand.

As calm eventually came on her again, she walked back over the grassy rise that led down into the yard. Harry Edwards, the reporter from the *Argus*, was bundled up in a scarf and brown wool coat and was seated at a small table on the porch and writing notes. He was the reporter Eva had felt the easiest with and on a whim she approached him.

'Good afternoon, Mr Edwards.'

He looked up, and stood when he saw it was her.

'Miss Carmichael.'

'Please sit down, Mr Edwards. I've just been walking for a while and I think it's blown out a few cobwebs.'

'It's cold out, Miss.'

'I became very used to the outside air at sea,' she said, and she half smiled. 'It's harder to get my land legs to work actually. What are you writing?'

'Oh, just notes. To myself, really.'

Eva sat at the rickety table. She fiddled with the bandage on her hand. The raw skin under it was healing, and was tight and itchy.

'Could I read your notes?' she asked him.

Edwards hesitated, as though trying to remember if there was anything there she should not read. He turned his journal around and slid it over to her.

Three bodies were recovered on Sunday and one more yesterday. The bodies were Miss Eva Carmichael's sister Raby, and their mother Rebecca, plus the two men Miss Carmichael told me about who washed near the mouth of the gorge on the spar with her, and who then swam away. They were Mr Reginald Jones and Mr Arthur Mitchell.

The tide has taken away the other bodies that the survivors saw on the beach that day. Another was seen to westward but the cliffs are two hundred feet high there and run straight down to the water.

Note: Mr Blyth, representing the shipping agents said that even though much cargo has floated in, much never will as it will either be too heavy or cannot escape the hull.

Eva and Harry looked up suddenly. Hooves were clattering up the winding drive and the horses turned in towards the stables.

Three riders. They could have news.

Gibson leapt from his horse and tossed the reins to Jack and growled an order at him. The other two men were Mr Blyth and George Ford.

Gibson and Blyth headed towards the house.

'I'll go ask if you like,' Harry offered. He walked about ten paces and met them in the yard. Then Tom came out of the house. He had not gone out that morning due to a terrible headache.

'Has something happened, Mr Gibson?' Harry Edwards asked and Eva was able to hear him clearly. She kept still though. They did not seem to see her in the porch shadow and for once she wanted to hear the unfiltered news.

'Interesting cargo came in, Harry. The constable guarding the top of the cliff spotted it nosing its way into the gorge. Couldn't miss it. Huge crate. Must mean the hull has breached further. They managed to catch it as it washed into the shallows.

'What was in the crate?'

'Not open yet, but the stamp says something about a Melbourne exhibition.'

'I know what that'll be,' Tom said. A green kerchief was knotted at his neck. 'A peacock sculpture. Pretty valuable I heard.'

'Well, valuable or not,' Blyth said. 'There's a syndicate that's just bought salvage rights and everything'll belong to them now.'

'That reminds me, Tom,' Gibson said. 'I got Mr Blyth's permission to bring one thing up from the gorge.' He marched back to his horse and retrieved an item from his saddle bag. It was square and flat and wrapped in hessian.

He passed the item to Tom. 'I'm guessing this is yours.' His smile was weary, satisfied, cautious.

Tom unwrapped the hessian and took out a broken panel of wood and Eva read it easily from where she sat. In black, stencilled letters "…EARCE" stood out on the green paint.

'It's from the lid of my sea chest,' Tom said.

'Was there anything valuable inside?' Harry asked.

Tom hesitated.

'Memories mostly. Letters, a book.' He gazed in the direction of a distant bird call. 'My diary and my father's diary. And … my stepfather's watch. Otherwise just clothes and odd things.' He ran his hand over the remains of his name. 'Thanks for this. When I get a new sea chest, I'll keep it inside.'

Gibson shuffled his feet tiredly.

'If you can manage it, Tom,' he said, 'we're taking the hay cart to the gorge in about ten minutes, and tools. The bodies are still in the cave. They're well wrapped and it's cold there, but we have to get them up to be buried, tomorrow preferably. We've enough wreckage washed in to build two reasonable coffins – one for the women, one for the men.'

Tom glanced down at the piece of wood in his hand.

'I'll fetch my coat.' Tom turned away and his eyes met Eva's at the porch, and he paled.

The men followed his gaze.

Eva raised her hand to Tom. 'I'm alright,' she said. She watched Gibson and Blyth look at each other. They nodded to her and went into the house.

While Harry returned to the porch, she felt her heart beating hard. A burial. Tomorrow.

But a thought crept into her mind.

'Mr Edwards,' she said as he sat. 'Mrs Gibson said yesterday that a reward should go to Tom. Could you mention to the authorities that they consider the gift of a watch to replace the one he lost from his sea chest?'

Harry wrote a quick note in the margin of his journal.

'Consider that done, Miss Carmichael.'

'The burial tomorrow. I suppose you'll write about that too.' It wasn't a question. 'Could I read it before you send it off please?'

He nodded. 'Of course.'

The next day throughout the burial, Lavinia stayed close to Eva. Many locals came, plus all the reporters and Mr Blyth. Two coffins were taken in the hay cart to a place westward of the gorge overlooking the section of ocean where the *Loch Ard* had sunk. Eva could not comprehend how the bodies and coffins had been lifted from the beach. She looked out at what she could see of the rugged coast. Seeing and hearing it again made her legs weak.

Workers from nearby farms had dug two deep holes.

Lavinia passed a small basket to Eva.

'You don't need to unless you want to,' she said.

Eva looked in the basket. Petals of roses and early wildflowers. Handfuls of lavender and rosemary. Two men stood beside the coffins with hammers in their hands, waiting.

'They've left the lid of your family's coffin loose in case you want to spread petals.' Lavinia looked Eva in the eyes. 'I asked them to cover the faces with black veils, because …'

Eva nodded.

'The damage,' she said.

'Yes,' Lavinia said.

'I can do it.'

The men lifted the lid aside. Two bodies lay tightly beside each other. They looked smaller. Raby was still in her green, velvet dress. Her mother in black. The clothes were ripped, and sandy. There was a strong smell of decay. Even in winter, five days was too long. Blowflies buzzed hungrily.

Eva straightened her back. Held her breath, and quickly littered handfuls of petals over the two most important women in her world.

Hammers. Ropes. The coffins being lowered as Mr McIntyre, the chaplain, read out the service. Just one hymn… *The Lord's my Shepherd*, Psalm 23. Shovels.

That afternoon, Eva looked for Harry Edwards and found him again on the porch.

'You're here to read my notes, Miss Carmichael?'

'If you don't mind Mr Edwards. It's helping me see things through others' eyes.'

He looked at her amazed. 'It's never occurred to me that my writing could be helpful to the grieving.' He turned his journal towards her.

The coffins had initials carved into them – on one "M.C., 46" for Mrs Carmichael, and "R.C., 21" for her daughter Rebecca, who Miss Eva calls Raby. The other coffin showed "R.J., 28" for the man Jones, and "A.M." with no age for the other man, Mitchell.

Mr Gibson arranged small crosses for the graves until headstones could be delivered from Melbourne. All just in time too because the weather was changing. The wind had begun to gust, probably around twenty knots, and heavy black clouds darkened the sky to the west and south. A reminder of the violence of this piece of coast.

Eva was with Tom when he wrote a telegram to his mother in San Francisco:

MOTHER. IN ALL THE NEWSPAPERS. MY SHIP LOCH ARD SANK SOUTH OF VICTORIA. I AM SAFE. WILL WRITE WHEN I CAN. TOM.

On Monday 10 June, a telegram arrived at Glenample from Tom's mother, under her maiden name Emily Mayne, and Tom read it quietly to Eva.

THANK YOU FOR TELEGRAM. I RECEIVED NEWSPAPER CLIPPING FROM COUSIN IN NEXT COUNTY. THANKING GOD YOU AND GIRL SAFE. PROUD OF YOU. PLEASE WRITE SOON. MOTHER.

CHAPTER FORTY

Tuesday 11 June
Glenample
Eva

The first week staggered into the second at the Gibson's place. Eva saw men cloaked against the weather drive wagons past the gates. They carried signed documents that proved their salvage rights, and they carted away from the gorge what they could.

The last few journalists lingered on at Glenample.

Eleven days after the wreck, Eva sat at Lavinia's desk and gazed out the window. For once, she was letting the horrid loss and darkness break into her day.

Three newspapers lay before her, slammed shut. Shunted together in a bitter pile.

The *Geelong Advertiser*. The *Camperdown Chronicle*. The *Argus*.

The wind rattled windows. It bent distant trees. Rain beat on the tin roof and slanted across the muddy yard and filled holes with water and cut narrow ruts into the slopes beyond.

The three remaining reporters smoked their pipes in the sheltered section of the porch. They annoyed her. Everyone annoyed her.

'Morning, Eva,' Tom said cheerily as he came through the doorway.

Irritation prickled through Eva and she leapt up from her chair.

'Mr Pearce,' she said, using his title for the first time since he had dragged her from the ocean.

Her face felt like iron and her cheekbones hurt.

His expression crashed from kind to confused.

She stabbed her hands onto her hips.

'It's too much! Why won't they leave us alone? Do you know that some newspapers are even suggesting romance, and that you and I should marry?' She raised her voice against the noise of rain on the roof. 'Why don't you send those men away?'

Tears flooded from her eyes and she felt them hot on her face. She pressed her handkerchief onto each cheek. She looked at the handkerchief. The daisies embroidered in the corner stood out as a strong reminder that almost nothing she owned now was hers. She had, in a gifted dilly bag in her room, a few other things retrieved from her father's desk that had washed in – damaged photographs, and some papers he had hidden in a rubber cushion. Everything else was gone.

'Why Tom?' Her sharp voice surprised even herself, but she didn't care.

Tom took a careful step forward. He looked older today.

Her throat thickened. This was the lowest she'd felt since the burial – publicly at least.

'What did we do so wrong?' She flung a hand in the air. 'Why did God let it happen? And why couldn't you sailors launch the lifeboats in time?'

He stood there.

She yelled. 'You should have left me to die!' Her heart was pounding. 'And you …' she slammed her hand onto the tea-table beside her, and it hurt. And it frightened her more than him. 'You're the hero. The mighty one. But you've not lost your family!'

She stopped solid.

She knew almost nothing of Tom's family – who they were; where they were, except that his mother was somewhere in America.

Tom took another step closer.

'I don't know why we were saved,' he whispered. Eva suddenly sensed, due to the unusual silence, that others in the house had become alert to the change of mood.

He scraped a chair from beside the little table and turned it, nodding for her to sit. She sank into it miserably.

Then he pulled another chair in front of her and sat down. She had never noticed the deep darkness of his eyes.

'I can't answer your questions,' Tom said. 'I wish I could. But I can tell you a bit about how I think about it.' His face filled with emotion. He took a slow long breath.

'Our voyage was three months. We travelled maybe a third of the way around the earth. It's a huge planet of land, and of oceans that no one can tame. At any one moment, there's a storm in one place, a becalming somewhere else.'

He looked out the window.

'And there'll be warm summer breezes somewhere, heat in the south, blizzards on lands in the north. And all these things can happen at the same exact moment in time. All I know, Eva, is that if we can blame God for the bad things, then we can also choose to be grateful for the good.'

He stood and walked to the window and leaned his hands on the side of the frame. The slate sky outside silhouetted his body.

'Sometimes,' Tom went on, 'we have to find a way to accept that what happens is what happens. We're alive – here, today in this room – and somehow, in your way and mine, we can each find a way to make the best of it.'

Shame stung Eva. She inhaled and tried to settle herself. She hunted inside herself for a patch of calm but her body trembled all over.

'Tom, I know you're right. But I don't know how to make the best of this.' She dabbed away the tears on her cheeks. 'And I'm sorry for what I said.'

'I know.' His fingers touched on the kerchief at his throat. 'It's fine.'

'Please,' she begged. 'Tell me about your family. Maybe it will help me too.'

He returned to the chair in front of her. His face lengthened. Relaxed. He answered.

'My father died when I was fourteen, and my mother remarried. Sadly, the man she married – he was Captain Robert Pearce – died a year later in a shipwreck.' He paused. 'But I was still keen to become a sailor. Eventually, my mother took my three sisters and my brother to live in America with relatives. I guess she couldn't bring herself to live in Australia anymore.' He shrugged and Eva swallowed a lump. She felt sad for him, for his losses long before hers.

The fire in the kitchen crackled. The cook scraped the grate closed and stirred something in a pot. A gamey aroma of mutton stew with rosemary percolated through the rooms. In the gumtrees outside, Eva heard a mudlark call. Another replied. On the porch, the reporters had stuffed more tobacco into their pipes and wandered off out of sight.

'It seems we've had to grow up early, the two of us,' Eva said quietly.

Tom nodded. His brown eyes locked onto hers.

'I'm not sure if this'll help, but your brother Thomas asked me back at the start of our voyage about why I was a sailor. Before I thought much about it I told him it was because sailing was my place in the world. What I meant was that sailing is where I fit – it's where I'm comfortable, for now at least. You fitted with your family and where they were going, but that's changed now. One day you'll find your place again. It might be a choice you make or you might one day find yourself right there, and somehow you'll just know.'

Eva said nothing. Tom's words were helping a few of the fragments fall into place in her mind, making a little more sense out of the many bits of horrible.

'This may be the wrong time to tell you,' Tom said, 'but I'll probably leave for Melbourne next week. If you need me to stay longer, I will. But at some point, I'd like to get to the Loch Line's company office to find out how to get on with my apprenticeship.'

Another change. But she knew neither of them could stay there forever.

'I understand. Of course, you must go.' Then something leapt into her mind.

'Tom! I've had no news of my brother William. When you're in Melbourne, could you try to find him? He's a sailor like you and is working somewhere there. He's the only one left in my family.'

'Of course,' Tom said.

'He works for the same shipping agent who managed the *Loch Ard*. The last letter from William said he was working in one of the warehouses between voyages. We've already telegrammed twice, and I even asked Mr Blyth when he was here. He said he'd ask someone in the office to look up William's records but I've heard nothing yet. I have a feeling the salvaging is a whole lot more important to Mr Blyth and it could be ages before I hear anything.'

'I'll make it a priority to look for him when I'm in Melbourne. When I find him, shall I send him to you here?'

'Yes please. The Gibsons have offered for me to stay as long as I want. I'm waiting to hear from my uncle about my passage back to Ireland. I imagine I'll be here a few more weeks at least.'

She gazed out the window. The agitation was easing. Her eyes were drying.

'Tom, I'm sorry for being angry.'

'Let's not talk about it anymore. Think about William coming to visit you.'

'And on that,' Eva said, 'one thing puzzles me.' Her eyes washed over the pile of newspapers on Lavinia's desk. 'With so many stories in all the papers about the *Loch Ard*, and particularly with all our names listed, William has not sent a message or tried to visit me. It's not a secret where I am.'

CHAPTER FORTY-ONE

Tuesday 18 June
Tom

Tom sat beside the window in the carriage at Colac Station. The train was headed to Geelong then Melbourne, to arrive that evening. Outside, steam billowed about the platform and puffed across the faces of the dozen or so folk standing there.

He brushed some horse hair off the knee of his new black moleskin trousers. He wore a new white woollen shirt too, and a blue woollen jacket, and sturdy leather work-boots. All had been bought from a fund that hundreds of people from the area had given to help him and Eva to replace their possessions. In the rack above his head was a new canvas bag with two leather handles and wooden toggles to close it. In its bottom was the scrap from his sea chest. Next to it, carefully folded, was Straz's kerchief. Above them, a full change of new clothes.

A few days earlier, Hugh Gibson had taken him to the tiny store beside the Post Office at Port Campbell to buy these things. Lavinia Gibson had spent that afternoon shortening the sleeves of the jacket and the trousers.

Sitting in the carriage now, it ached that he was leaving Eva. And the Gibsons. Hugh had offered to escort Tom to Melbourne. Tom said no.

He deliberately did not look out the window at the little crowd bunched together. There was nothing he could express through dusty glass.

A folded newspaper was on his lap. The *Camperdown Chronicle*. Hugh had bought it from the newsstand then pointed out another mention of the hero. Tom's eyes skimmed, instead, the ads for potato prices, and sewing machine repairs, and the chemist offering to pull teeth with or without ether spray.

That "hero" the journalists wrote about did not get it right. He did not get the lifeboats out. He did not save Straz. He mistook Eva's cries for a seagull. He nearly forgot to mark the gorge before he went for help.

And beyond worse. In the hours before the *Loch Ard* wrecked, he might have prevented it all.

When he had smelled something different that evening, he had not thought any more about it. He should have dug deeper. He should have realised that after three months at sea and smelling salt and ocean, that the smell of eucalyptus and red earth and sheoaks was as clear as black was against white.

No hero. He felt more like a fraud and it was why he had not told anyone since then about the smell. He would one day, and he wished Straz was there. They'd grown to trust one another after Straz's stowaway cousin had been revealed.

So, sitting there waiting for the train to leave, he had a conversation in his mind with Straz about the smell of Australia.

And he heard Straz's answer as clear as day.

'Are you serious? You're not the only one who'd have noticed it. You're not the only one who knew what Australia smelled like. And even if you'd said something, do you think Mac and the capt'n would've changed course after them taking all those readings and checking the chart? Maybe. But not for ages. Not till after they'd done it all again and again. Get over it Tom. You're alive, with your life ahead of you. Go on now and do it.'

A kookaburra yakkered in a tree beyond. Perhaps it was heralding more rain. A cold, white sky trickled light through the train window. The buildings outside cast no shadows.

Three others sat in Tom's compartment. Opposite him, a woman and boy. The boy's left arm was bandaged from elbow to fingertips. He held a painted wooden soldier in his right hand. Going to a hospital for an operation apparently.

And a reporter from the *Melbourne Age* sat beside Tom. The reporter had been at Glenample with the others and, by chance, or not, was leaving on the same train as Tom.

The whistle blew. The wheels screeched. The train inched forward. Eva took a few steps alongside. She waved a lace handkerchief. Tom ached. He leaned forward and forced a smile and waved.

Half an hour into the journey, the reporter eased out his notebook.

'May I ask about …?'

But Tom looked at him then turned his face to the window. When Tom next glanced around, the notebook and pencil were gone. He closed his eyes.

The carriage leaned into a corner then straightened.

A mast scraped on the edge of a cliff. It shot sparks into the air.

The noise Tom jolted awake. The scrape was the train's wheels. His skin stung with sweat. The others had nodded off too and he forced himself to take calming breaths until his thumping heart slowed. Visions came of a spar falling, of Captain Gibb bawling out orders, of Evory and Thomas Carmichael trying to release a lifeboat, of Straz's green kerchief appearing hours later from Tom's trouser pocket. His heart pounded and sweat prickled his forehead. He slumped back into his corner.

Just before six, the train clicked into Geelong Station for its scheduled forty-five-minute stop.

'What's that fuss about?' the woman opposite asked. She craned her neck and looked at what was happening outside.

Crammed along the cold platform were several dozen young women straining eyes and bodies to see into each compartment as the train squealed to its stop.

It would be good to get out for some fresh air. Tom stepped out behind the others from his carriage onto the platform and a man's voice called out, 'Tom?'

Quite naturally, Tom turned his head towards the voice. And regretted it. It was a trick.

The press of women screamed and moved as one towards him. Someone yelled out, 'Brave Tom Pearce! – Brave Tom Pearce!'

He cringed and tried to look past them for a place to hide.

The Gentlemen's room? Or perhaps he could just get back onto the train, but they could easily follow him.

Someone must have telegrammed ahead from Colac.

Girls in winter cloaks with muffs and gloves shoved envelopes at him, begging for his autograph. He smiled for their sakes but, without signing them, he pressed the envelopes gently back. The burly, uniformed station master pushed in, gripped Tom by his upper arm and dragged him towards the station entrance.

'I'll get you away from this,' he said into Tom's ear. A minute later they were in a wagon, and three minutes later they were in the restaurant of a hotel called the Black Bull.

'I was wondering who they were waiting for,' the station master said, after a long pull on his beer. 'Not much exciting usually happens at Geelong Station.'

Tom wondered if he'd have to answer questions but the food arrived and the station master dived into it ravenously.

'Thanks,' Tom said.

The station master grunted. Maybe he rescued passengers every day. Maybe it was how he escaped for his supper.

The food was good. The beer was better. Then Tom realised that the train's next stop would be in Melbourne, and that the Geelong platform was probably a warning of what might wait for him there.

As if he'd read Tom's mind, the station master sipped his beer then asked him, 'Who's collecting you in Melbourne?'

'Oh, my Uncle Edgar.'

'Know his address? I'll telegram ahead and arrange a back door at the station.'

Tom knew the address. His mother's sister, Doreen, had lived with them for a while and when Doreen had married, she'd moved into a house only a few streets from theirs.

The station master pulled a notebook from his pocket.

'I'd be very grateful. My uncle is Edgar Williams at Flinders House in Canterbury Road, Toorak.'

Thirty-five minutes after they'd escaped, they were back at the train. The crowd on the platform had doubled.

'Excuse me,' Tom said, a lot. He ignored questions and squeals. He leapt through the first door he could get to and walked through three carriages to reach his own. Quickly he pulled the curtains closed then dropped onto his seat.

The woman and child stared at him. The journalist entered, gave a quick embarrassed nod to Tom, then fell immediately into a fake sleep.

'Mister, is it really you?' the boy asked.

The mother patted her son's leg. 'Shush, Bobby.'

'It's alright,' Tom said. He smiled at the boy. An audience of one was not so terrible, so he answered a few questions then said goodnight.

Late that night, the train slowed into Melbourne's Spencer Street Station. It juddered to a stop. Tom eased open an inch of curtain to look out. If he'd had any hope that the lateness of their arrival might limit the number of people, it disappeared immediately.

Hundreds, mostly women, jostled one another and cheered as a final blast of steam filled the freezing air. Envelopes flapped over their heads like butterflies on a forgotten cabbage patch.

The conductor opened the door from the passage. He steered the disappointed reporter and his luggage out of the compartment, and helped the woman with her suitcase and her child. As he left, he leaned back towards Tom.

'Mr Pearce, stay put please.' Minutes later, he hurried back.

'Right, be quick. Got your bag? They've organised an exit for you. Bet you didn't expect this sort of attention when you left London?'

'So true,' Tom said.

The conductor led Tom towards the rear of the train then out the guard's door onto the tracks. It was pitch black except for a dull glow from the conductor's lantern. Tom followed him along the tracks to a service platform.

'Good to see you my boy!' came a familiar voice.

'Uncle Edgar! Thank goodness.'

'Good luck!' the conductor said.

'We'll need to be quick, lad,' Uncle Edgar said. 'It won't take them long to figure you're gone, and they'll be out of that building in a flash. I've got a cab outside.' He took Tom's bag.

Gas lamps lit the street alongside the station. Uncle Edgar led Tom to the cab. He tossed Tom's bag onto the seat.

Someone screamed from the station entrance, 'Is that him?'

Tom jumped into the cab and Uncle Edgar almost landed on him in the rush.

'Go!' Uncle Edgar yelled to the driver. 'Whew,' he said. 'I didn't expect that much excitement to end the day.'

They clattered along streets that were wet with earlier rain and dark except for misty glows on gas-lit corners. Soon they were in the suburbs and in a short time they were at the house.

Aunt Doreen had raisin cake on a glass plate, and the kettle steaming on the stove for tea. She looked a lot like Tom's mother but younger and a lot less worn.

After a quick welcome, she poured boiling water into the teapot.

'Tom,' she said. She sounded worried. 'What a time you've had. How …?'

Uncle Edgar interrupted. 'Dear, we should save our questions. Maybe tomorrow.'

And soon afterwards Tom was laying in the dark looking at the night sky through the bedroom window, and trying to fall asleep.

When he woke in morning, he smelled bacon. Halfway through his fried breakfast, someone knocked on the front door.

CHAPTER FORTY-TWO

Wednesday 19 June 1878
Tom

'A telegram for you,' Uncle Edgar said, laying it on the table beside Tom.

Tom used a striped napkin to wipe the crumbs from his mouth. He opened the envelope.

The Executive Council Chamber.
An invitation to Thomas Pearce to a special presentation.
By the Governor of Victoria.
Three o'clock today at the Treasury.

He read the paragraph underneath, then passed it across the table. Aunt Doreen dabbed her hands on her apron and read silently over Uncle Edgar's shoulder. Tom looked at the clock on the mantelpiece. He couldn't risk going to the shipping company now. He'd have to queue and there'd be forms to fill, and he'd already been told, being the only crewman to survive the disaster, that he'd have to be interviewed further regarding everything that happened before and during the wreck. With no Captain's logbook to prove anything, Tom's word was the only evidence.

Whatever was planned at the Treasury, he had a feeling word would already be out. He could have the same problems as the previous night.

'If you don't mind,' Uncle Edgar said, 'I'll come with you. I've taken the day off work.'

'Why don't you try to enjoy it?' Aunt Doreen asked. 'Sign autographs. Shake hands.'

'Maybe,' Tom said. 'But I only came to Melbourne to sign back onto a ship. Journalists have been around me for two weeks, even on the train yesterday. It's not what I'm used to.'

None of it was.

Uncle Edgar said nothing, but at two-thirty a cab waited outside their door.

They drove through streets Tom recognised. Past buildings he knew well. And they walked up the stone steps into the Treasury without encountering even one excited young woman.

A clerk led them in and to a door marked "Executive Council Chamber".

'Wait here, please,' he said.

'Relieved?' Uncle Edgar asked.

'I think so,' Tom said. 'So far.'

They were invited in.

There was murmuring and shuffling of carved and cushioned chairs from around a long, polished table.

More than a dozen black-coated government men stood up from their chairs. A small contingent of journalists lingered at the far end. Tom recognised Harry Edwards who'd been at Glenample.

'They're probably only here if they promised not to let the word out before,' Uncle Edgar whispered.

Tom nodded. One relief swapped for another dread.

The clerk announced, 'Mr Thomas Pearce, and Mr Edgar Williams,' then left.

A few men looked surprised. Their eyes went from Tom to his uncle. Back to Tom. They'd probably expected someone with more presence, taller perhaps. Someone who looked like a hero not an unremarkable man-boy sailor.

'Welcome, Mr Pearce,' said a gentleman halfway along the table. 'I'm Sir George Bowen, Governor of Victoria.' He was square faced. A strong voice came from a sturdy torso. 'And on behalf of the Government of Victoria, I have great pleasure in presenting you,' and he took a wooden box from the man on his left, 'with this watch. It's a slight token of the respect and admiration in which your noble conduct is held by all classes in the colony.' He beckoned Tom to approach.

The box was smooth, and heavy. Tom thanked him and returned to stand with his uncle at the end of the table.

The ocean crashed through Tom's mind. He tried to listen. To concentrate.

Like a joke told in the wrong place, he remembered he needed to ask his uncle to take him to St Kilda's auction rooms to buy a replacement sea chest.

The governor's voice carried on. Then he paused. He glanced down at his speech on the table in front of him.

'So, err. It's hoped that while you have distinguished yourself by your gallant action, your example will stimulate to similar deeds the youth of this colony, which is proud of you.'

Journalists scribbled notes and Tom cringed at the Governor's final words that would make their way into newspapers. He had a feeling that many of the "youth of this colony" would resent a merchant sailor being put up to be an example to them.

The men around the room seemed to be waiting for him to speak.

Tom lifted the wooden lid. Inside a gold watch rested on red velvet, and a chain ran under the fabric. Tom slid a finger under the watch. Heavy for its size.

'Thank you,' he said. His voice carried across the room. 'And I hope I shall always do my duty towards my country.'

Two photographers came forward and asked Tom to pose for photographs.

'Lean on that,' one said.

'Sit there,' another asked.

Black cloths. Flashes. Forced smiles and poses. A headache began at the back of Tom's eyes.

Tom and his uncle returned to Flinders House and Tom's heart sank when he saw another telegram addressed to him on the kitchen table. He opened it.

'What?' Uncle Edgar asked.

'Tomorrow evening at eight o'clock at the Town Hall,' Tom said.

His name was a last-minute addition to the annual ceremony of bravery awards given out by the Humane Society of Victoria.

'I read about that in here,' Aunt Doreen said.

A copy of the *Argus* lay on the table. She flicked over the first few sheets then ran a finger down a column of advertisements.

'Here it is.' She turned the paper around for Tom and his uncle to read.

'Well, at least it's admission by ticket only,' said Tom.

He looked at his aunt.

'Aunt Doreen, please don't think I'm ungrateful. But the whole thing was just a terrible accident. Everyone did the best they could to help one another. I didn't do anything special. So many have died.'

'And I'm sure you miss them all, dear,' his aunt said.

'I'm taking tomorrow off too,' Uncle Edgar said. 'What do you need to do next, Tom?'

'Oh no!' Tom said. He pressed his hand onto his forehead. 'I'd entirely forgotten that Eva asked me to go to the shipping office to ask about her brother. Apart from that, I need to answer questions from the shipping company about the wreck, and to sort out my next ship.'

He ran his fingers through his hair.

'If there's time tomorrow, then maybe the auctions too?'

'What do you need from the auctions?'

'A replacement sea chest. I bought my last one cheap, and it came good after a coat of paint and some varnish.'

Uncle Edgar put his hand on the newspaper.

'Looks like this beast is your enemy and your friend. All the auctions are listed in here.'

CHAPTER FORTY-THREE

Monday 24 June 1878
Eva

Eva raised the newspaper from the desk. After reading the first part of an article, she grinned.

'He would have hated that so much.'

She read more and laughed.

'What's that, Eva?' Lavinia said behind her.

'It's an article about the bravery awards at the Town Hall last week. All that attention. Thousands of people there.'

Eva read aloud the paragraph.

'There was an immense attendance of the public, induced principally by the presentation of a gold medal to Thomas Pearce, who was greeted by the audience with tumultuous applause. The gold medal received by Mr Pearce was the first ever awarded by the society.'

'You're right,' Lavinia said. She laughed. 'He would have hated everything about it.'

'And there's a mention of me,' Eva said. 'The wish of some unprincipled photographers to make money out of the desire of the public to obtain portraits of Miss Carmichael and Mr Thomas Pearce, the only survivors from the *Loch Ard*, has led some of them to issue spurious likenesses.' She had to stop reading while she laughed out loud. '… And that those who purchase either of the portraits would only be throwing away their money.'

'Did you ever think people would sell counterfeit photos of you?' Lavinia asked, sinking to the couch.

'I wish I could see one of those "spurious likenesses" of Tom and me,' Eva said, laughing again.

Eva skimmed other articles of the *Geelong Advertiser*. She read more.

'And … five thousand tickets are in circulation, and judging from the demand today, twice that number would have been eagerly availed of by the Pearce-seeing public.'

'So, now it's the "Pearce-seeing public",' said Lavinia. 'They've named the crowd after him.'

Eva closed the newspapers. 'I miss him. I wonder when I'll hear from him again?'

An hour later a rider galloped into the yard with a telegram for Eva. There had been many from well-wishers and she nearly put it aside to read later. But something made her pick it up.

From Tom.

EVA. SO SORRY FOR THE FOLLOWING. WILLIAM CARMICHAEL DEPARTED SYDNEY ON THE SHIP ESSEX TO LONDON IN APRIL. SUGGEST YOU TELEGRAM FAMILY TO DISCOVER IF HE HAS CONTACTED THEM THERE. KIND THOUGHTS, TOM PEARCE.

'Lavinia,' Eva called towards the kitchen. 'Is the rider still here?'

'I believe he's feeding and watering his horse at the stable.' Lavinia came in and looked out the window into the yard. 'Is something wrong?'

'I need to telegram my uncle in Ireland.' She paused. 'William doesn't know. About anything.'

A breeze puffed at a large gum beyond the fence.

Eva could picture her younger brothers enjoying that tree. Evory would have sat with his back against the trunk to read a book, and Thomas would have climbed it to the very top. Margaret and Annie would pick wildflowers in the field beyond. Her mother would begin to plant a vegetable garden. Her father – he'd be sitting on the porch smoking his pipe and reading the latest medical journals. And Raby would probably be in her room gazing at herself in the mirror and waiting for the latest fashion catalogues to arrive.

But what about herself? Her parents could no longer make decisions for her. Where was she supposed to live? What was she supposed to do? She had William if she could find him, but he was a sailor.

Eva wrote a telegram to her uncle, telling him about William. She folded it and carried it to the kitchen and Lavinia sent Eliza out with it to the rider.

'Lavinia,' Eva said. 'I'd like to stay another couple of weeks if I can, then I want to visit Melbourne before I return to Ireland. I may as well see the city our family was going to spend a little time in.'

'Are you sure, Eva?'

It was the first time since the night before the shipwreck that Eva had been sure of anything.

'Entirely. And perhaps we could have lunch with Tom one day, if he's free.'

'I'll come with you then, to Melbourne. I haven't been shopping since last spring and I could show you the sights as well.'

'An adventure!' Eva thought. And then she thought, *Another adventure.*

For the rest of the day, Eva studied and memorised a map of Melbourne city.

CHAPTER FORTY-FOUR

Monday 5 August 1878
Eva

It was early afternoon and nine weeks since the wreck when Eva stood beside the ship taking her home to Ireland.

She had spent three weeks in Melbourne with Lavinia. Most days, they walked until they were footsore. They shopped for clothes and shoes and books. Numerous markets. Galleries. Coffee rooms. Even the Theatre Royal to see *Rag Fair*. They'd stayed in a private guest house under aliases to avoid the publicity that had hounded Tom earlier. And they'd even seen Tom once, when he had day leave from the shipping company where he was doing shore work until he sailed.

Eva was starting to feel she could think again. She coped in the daytimes. But some nights the numbing grief would shred her until she finally slept.

Lavinia had convinced her to wear a widow's veil over her face to disguise herself. Eva was glad too, when she saw photos of her and Tom for sale inside newsagent windows. Some clearly were fakes.

But on that pier at Hobsons Bay, she was not wearing the veil. Her name had been listed on the passenger manifests in the newspapers and a crowd of perhaps a hundred folk flustered around her and between the railway tracks and cargo-laden wagons.

A new sadness had been filling her for the past two days. She was saying goodbye to the Gibsons, and to Tom.

She wore new clothes. Her new luggage was loaded. And in her purse was the ticket taking her to England then to Ireland on the fast mail steamer *Tanjore*.

The ship would make mail stops on the way and Eva had memorised them all to distract herself from this very moment of parting – Glenelg in South Australia, Albany in Western Australia, Point de Galle in Ceylon, Bombay in India, then, after the Suez Canal, Venice in Italy.

But before any of that, the *Tanjore* would pass by the piece of coast where her mother and sister's grave looked out over the grave of the *Loch Ard*.

Young women from the crowd pressed silk scarves and linen handkerchiefs into Eva's hands as tokens of their thoughts, and the pile of fabrics grew so fast that Lavinia relieved Eva of most and stuffed them into her own basket.

Eva folded three silk scarves into the embroidered purse hanging from her wrist. Under the ticket, and at the bottom of her purse, was a telegram she'd finally received from William four weeks ago.

She had not replied. After William heard about the *Loch Ard*, he had boarded the first ship leaving England and was right then sailing to Melbourne. He would go to pay his respect at the graves. She would see him in Dublin when he returned.

The crowd crushed in and someone fell against Eva, almost knocking her hat off. Hugh's face reddened in anger, but he turned with Tom and they used their arms to back the crowd away.

Tom pleaded, 'Please let Miss Carmichael have some final minutes with her friends.'

'We love you Tom!' a girl called. A few others laughed happily. But gradually they eased back and Tom turned to Eva. There was a tenderness in his face that Eva hadn't seen before.

'How long before you sail?' she asked him.

'Five days,' he said, croakily. 'On the *Loch Sunart*.'

A whistle blew. The ship's bell rang.

'It's time,' Hugh said.

'Thank you, for everything,' Eva said to the Gibsons. Emotion rose inside her.

'I'm not sure how I'd have coped … if I'd not been in the care of such wonderful people.' Her face filled.

Lavinia held her tightly then let go.

'Eva.' Tom took her hands and held them. His touch calmed her.

'Tom,' she said, taking a deep breath. 'I'm going to work out where my place is in the world.'

Tom's lips parted to say something but he closed them and his eyes moistened.

'Thank you, Tom,' Eva said. 'I'll pray for you every day.' They embraced. Eva walked up the wooden ramp. The captain greeted her and introduced her to the purser who led her to the companionway that led to the cabins. She turned then, and waved at her three friends, almost lost in the crowd.

In late September in Dublin, the day after Eva arrived, her frail, grieving grandmother gave her a sealed envelope with a scrawled redirection address from the Carmichael's old home.

In the small guest room of her Uncle Nicholas's home, Eva sat alone and read the letter. It was dated 1 April. William had sent it from Melbourne a month after the Carmichaels had sailed.

The letter made Eva realise that if they had known William was returning to Ireland to visit, they may have waited to see him. And the Carmichael family would now be alive and complete.

There was another letter from William. More recent and from after William finally heard about the wreck. Eva opened it flat and her eyes traced the words again. He had written it to Eva.

Even after the terrible shock I've had, and the terrible experiences you've had, I must say now how so proud I am of you, dear Eva, and so grateful to the midshipman who rescued you.

He explained at the end of the letter that he had taken care of their father's affairs and applied for probate through their solicitor, and that there was little money because most of their possessions had been sold before the voyage. Their father had taken away the value with him, now lost in the ocean. The few credit notes found inside a rubber cushion from the *Loch Ard* were in Eva's hat trunk. There were barely legible and would need to be considered by a court.

Inside her mind, Eva could almost hear her father asking mathematics questions of her, forcing her to think harder, work harder. To find a way around the next problem. It was the problem of her future.

During the six weeks on the *Tanjore*, Eva had thought about her future a lot.

Now, finally back where she could start again, she began to write a list of every opportunity she could imagine, even if it was reckless.

As she wrote, she smiled to herself and thanked Tom for showing her how to live again.

THE END

EPILOGUE 1 – TOM

December 1878
Leith, Scotland

Tom's voyage on the *Loch Sunart* was uneventful and they reached Gravesend near London in good time.

It was on the ship's outward journey from Gravesend, carrying passengers and cargo to Glasgow, that a gale howled over the north of England and blew anything that had braved the North Sea towards the rocky coast of Norway. On the ship, all hands fought the lines to tack back towards Scotland but, just when it seemed they were free, the wind swung viciously to the north.

A gust snapped a yard arm from the main mast and the arm fell and pierced the deck. No one was injured except the man who succeeded in lashing a line to a capstan as the yard arm fell. His action saved the timber from going through the decks and holing the hull. But the rope shredded the crewman's hands. The rest of the crew controlled the ship until the gale slackened. The captain decided they should dock in Leith to allow carpenters to make the repairs and to summon a doctor for the crewman.

Tom had been promoted to third-mate and his heart leapt when he heard the ship would stop in Leith. Minutes after the announcement, he begged use of the captain's charts. He ran his finger over one.

Leith dock was close to North Leith, the location of Straz's family at the Star Bank Inn. Straz had talked a lot about his family and over the months since the wreck of the *Loch Ard* Tom had searched the bank in his brain for every memory he could find from his time with Straz.

When Tom explained his reason for needing a few hours off in Leith, Captain Weir agreed easily. He knew the story of the *Loch Ard*.

Tom approached Star Bank Inn, a place he discovered was well known to all on the docks.

It was nearly evening. Along the path that separated the sea wall from the inn, a man was lighting the gaslights one by one.

The inn's door squeaked when Tom pushed on it. Inside, oil lamps hung from hooks in the ceiling and draped yellow light into the corners. A man served a whiskey each to two well-dressed men at the bar. Further along a boy around twelve polished the oak bar with a fistful of flannel. The boy … his eyes … his stance. The way he moved his shoulders as he cleaned.

This had to be Straz's younger brother.

Tom looked from the boy to the man and as he did the older man's eyes connected with his.

'Coom in. Coom in.' A strong Scottish roll. The voice of someone who had never stepped outside his homeland, and probably even his town, in all his life. The man beckoned and the two well-dressed customers glanced back then paid their attention to their whiskeys and their conversation.

Tom found the biggest gap between people at the bar. He pulled a shilling from his pocket.

The older man shuffled along to him. 'What can I get you, lad?' He wore a check shirt and cotton trousers. A scrap of teacloth draped over a shoulder. He had probably shaved two days ago for church.

Tom's plan had ended at the inn's door. Should he order a drink first?

'Are you Mr Strasenburgh?' he asked, his heart thumping solidly against his ribs.

'Aye. Aye. How can I 'elp ye?'

'If you're the father of a sailor named Robert, I'd like to talk with you. When it's convenient, sir.'

The man seemed to weaken at his knees and his hands dropped heavily onto the bar. Ridges furrowed above his eyes.

'What's wrong, Da?' It was the Robert look-alike. Mr Strasenburgh said nothing.

Tom glanced at the boy then back at Straz's father. 'Mr Strasenburgh. My name's Tom. I was on Robert's ship.'

Mr Strasenburgh stared at Tom.

'Will!' he said to the boy. 'Get George to coom watch the bar.' He grasped Tom's arm, as though he was stopping him from running away. 'Now, you coom round back 'ere Tom. Mary's oot back with the chil'ren.'

The smells of meats roasting and vegetables boiling for the customers filled the back room of the inn. Tom was soon in the kitchen perched on a stool with an ale in his hand. The shilling had been forced back into his pocket.

Mrs Strasenburgh was an aproned, nervous woman and Robert's father steered her towards a chair then stood behind her, leaning on the chair back. Two teenage girls lingered near the wall, and Straz's young brother Will hovered near the door.

'Mary,' Mr Strasenburgh said. 'This boy Tom knew our Rob. Tom, this is my wife Mary, and our daughters Edith and Beatrice. And this is our son Will. This is all our family, except

Robert. Please tell us aboot 'im. What 'appened there, on the ship?' His eyes were alight with hope and Tom saw that they knew they were looking at someone who had been with their son since they'd last seen him themselves.

So, Tom put the ale on the table and told it all backwards. He told how Robert spent his last minutes desperately working to free a lifeboat to try and keep the women and children safe. He told how he saw Robert – and he chose the words carefully – "fall asleep" in the ocean and how he tried to save him. He had to stop talking for a minute because he could not talk. Being there, in that room. All feeling exploded. It hurt.

Then he told of their friendship during the voyage. Their competitions. How Robert had helped the stowaway cousin. And it was new pain for the Strasenburgh family. No one had known what had happened to Cousin Jimmy until then.

Robert's parents wiped away tears. They smiled at the stories.

'Typical of our Rob. He was always competing with his friends,' Mrs Strasenburgh said. Her eyelashes glistened and grey hair wisped from under her headscarf.

'And 'elping folk,' said Mr Strasenburgh. 'Even when it meant breaking rules.'

'I have this,' Tom said.

He got off the stool.

He pulled the kerchief from his pocket and passed it, folded, to Robert's mother who looked at it then pressed it to her cheek. One of the girls gasped.

'Oy, Edith,' Will said. 'That's the kerchief you gave Rob.'

Edith was the older of Robert's sisters. She was slender with a square face and soft eyes. Lamplight glided over Edith's hair, and glinted off the dark-brown strands.

'You should keep it Eady,' Mrs Strasenburgh said. Edith rounded the table. Her mother raised the kerchief to her and it unfurled over Edith's open palm. Flowing green. Like the deep ocean grave that had grasped Straz and all that the *Loch Ard* held that night.

Edith held the kerchief in her hand. Her eyes asked a silent question but then she asked it aloud.

'He always wore this,' she said. A hint of hardness crept into her voice. 'But we heard they didn't recover his body. How did you get it?'

Something changed in the room. Tom suddenly wanted to take a step back. But he put his glass aside and squatted forward in front of Robert's mother so his eyes were level with hers. He gave his answer to Mrs Strasenburgh rather than to Edith.

He started to say to her, 'I tried …' but, as the words came out, a mop of sadness rose through his chest and neck. 'He was unconscious. There was too much debris. Too much water. When I reached out to pull him up, this was all that was left in my hand.' Tears swelled onto his cheeks. He looked at the floor. 'I couldn't find him,' he whispered.

Tom took a deep breath and stood. He slapped the dampness off his face. The boy Will planted his feet wide and folded his arms across his chest. It was like he was locking in all his pain.

'You survived!' he said. 'You should've got Rob out too.'

'Will!' his father growled. 'We 'ear of shipwrecks all the time from sailors. Survivors coom 'ere stowed oot with grief and guilt. We've all 'eard them talk. Tom 'ere would not have coom if he 'ad a thing to cover.'

'I think I should go,' Tom said. 'I'm sorry to have added to your sadness.' He began to move towards the door, to the bar, the outside, to his ship. Away from this loss and agony.

'No,' Mrs Strasenburgh said. 'You came to us. You'll eat and tell us everything you can remember about our Robert. We won't get this chance again.'

Over a supper of ham soup then pork chops, roasted potatoes, roasted apple, and boiled peas, Tom told the family his memories of their Robert. When he mentioned "Straz", his father laughed aloud.

'Straz is what boys called me, too, when I was young! Good to see the name passed on to my son.' He smiled but the expression washed away in the renewed memory that his son was gone.

Tom explained he'd be needed back on the ship. He rose and Straz's father shook his hand.

'Thank you, Tom, for cooming. You 'ad a choice and you didn't need to. It's appreciated.' Will shook Tom's hand too, and nodded a goodbye.

'Thank you, young man,' Straz's mother said. She hugged him and it was like she was trying to hold her son.

When Tom was out on the path, treading away into the night, footsteps came up behind him and he turned to face them.

A lamp light showed him it was Edith carrying the kerchief.

'Miss Edith!'

She puffed. 'Just call me Edith,' she said. 'Thank you for coming to see us Tom. It's hard for us, not having his body to bury. No grave to visit. Nothing except memories.' She held out the kerchief. 'Hearing your stories and seeing this, it's helped us all. It's true I gave it to Rob, but I want you to have it.'

Tom shook his head. 'I can't, Edith.'

'Please, Tom. Take it and you can make it up to me …
whenever you think of something else about Rob, write to me
and tell me, even if it's something bad he did.' She smiled a
sad smile. 'I'll only tell my family the good bits.'

Somehow, the kerchief remained in Tom's hand. Again.

'I will,' he promised.

'Stay safe, Tom,' Edith said. She turned and walked
back towards the glowing windows of Star Bank Inn.

Tom sensed something shift.

Could someone's place in the world change once more?

EPILOGUE 2 – EVA

Wednesday 12 December 1888
Wrington, Somerset

The morning the birth pains rose through her core and warned Eva her third baby would soon arrive, she was on her favourite sofa in their drawing room watching toddler Philip chase one-year-old Francis on hands and knees across the red Turkish rug, under a side table, and off towards the doorway into the hall. Both were squealing, but Eva knew there'd be wailing sometime soon. There always was.

Their maid dodged around them. She carried a small pile of letters across the room and placed them on the writing table beside Eva.

'Thank you, Mary,' Eva said.

'I'd best follow those two,' Mary said, 'until Hannah's free to watch them.' Hannah was a local girl they'd hired recently, and the boys loved her.

Eva smoothed her palm across her belly and felt a baby heel press hard under her ribs; she had decided months ago that this one needed to be a girl.

'Mary. You'd best send Bertie to get word to the midwife to come this afternoon please.'

Mary was a middle-aged spinster. Her pudginess hid her strength. Fussy. Reliable. Steel. Always in an ankle-length black skirt, white blouse, and dark jacket buttoned to her throat. Always properly mended, properly brushed and properly pressed.

'Oh! Mrs Eva! Is it time?' Her eyes were wide.

Eva nodded. 'Nothing to worry about. It's slow for now. Perhaps we should also send a telegram to the office to let Archie know. I don't want him to have a shock at supper.' Of all things, she'd married a man named Thomas as well. Thomas Achilles Townshend. But she called him Archie and he had warmed to the name quickly.

A yelp and crash came from the hall. Then a toddler-sized howl.

Mary strode out. Eva stood, leaned on the windowsill and clamped her teeth while a long pain burnt her belly. Her breaths began to take the familiar pattern of long and slow until calm returned. Then there was nothing except a tiny person stretching its limbs within her again.

She couldn't stand there waiting for each pain. Eva picked up the pile of letters and flicked through them until the masculine scrawl of one stopped her and spread a rare and warm smile across her face.

She flipped it over. T.R. Pearce.

It had been two years since she'd last heard from him, just after his wife, Edith, gave him a son they'd named Thomas. Eva gazed out the window.

This letter was the third he had written to her over the years, and she had replied each time. When Tom's first letter arrived, Archie had said, 'Your bond with him is proper, it's harmless, and you have my blessing. I'll be forever grateful to Tom Pearce that you're here with me.' His eyes were soft and genuine.

Eva unfolded the letter.

2 December 1888

Dear Eva
I hope you and your family are all in good health.
As before, my letter is to announce more good news at our home. I have another son, born in November. This boy we have named after my friend from the Loch Ard, who was also the older brother of my wife. My son's name is Robert Strasenburgh Pearce. He is dark featured with powerful lungs and firm little fists.
Do you remember my friend Robert?

Eva's mind searched the few faces she could recall from the ship, but a Robert? She was not sure if she remembered the name at all.

We called him 'Straz' and he and I were always competing, racing up the masts.

Eva frowned then burst out laughing, cut short by another pain.

Mary bundled in gripping Francis on her hip. 'Are you alright ma'am.'

Eva nodded. She breathed through the pain.

It took a long minute.

'Yes. Mary. I'm just reading a letter from a friend.'

Mary's face shaded. Eva was known to her household as "stern" so Mary would be confused to see her mistress in childbirth, and laughing.

'You should be lying down Mrs Eva. Let me help you to your room.'

But Eva had always stayed active during her labours, no matter what the midwives ordered. She remembered her father saying that women delivered healthier and quicker if they were upright as long as possible. 'They're not sick,' he used to say. 'And God gave us gravity for a reason. Why make a woman labour horizontally when she can go faster vertically?'

Her father …

Her children had no Carmichael grandparents, or aunts, or uncles except William. It was like staring into a black room.

'Mrs Eva?' Mary said into Eva's darkness.

'Oh, Mary. I'm fine. I'll just walk around in here for a while. And I'll ring the bell if it gets too much.'

So now I find myself with two sons, and I'm sure they'll be sailors too. Unless they follow after Edith's father and become innkeepers. I don't mind really. I'm so blessed with a good wife. My Edith works hard and raises young Tom well and somehow gets Robert to sleep peacefully. I cannot afford a maid, but Edith's family grew up without one and she does not complain at all.

How could a woman manage her home and children without a maid? Tom and Eva had truly been born into different worlds. But a miracle had put them on a ship, then in the ocean, then on a beach, then in the good hands of the Gibsons.

So many things could have gone wrong, but there she was, in a comfortable home with a caring husband, active boys, and hopefully a daughter before bedtime that night. She had fought off the sadness so many times that now, hidden inside her, was a loving but locked casket that held the memories of her parents, sisters and brothers.

I must sign off now dear Eva. I work for the Royal Mail Services from Southampton, and am due tomorrow to depart for the Brazils. Write when you can. Your letters remind me of how precious life is and how much we both might have missed out on.

God bless you
Your friend always
Thomas Richard Pearce (Tom)

The letter's arrival was good timing because she would be able to reply with her own news when she had regained strength in the coming days. Slowly, she read the letter twice more but then had trouble concentrating and pressed it onto the mantlepiece.

Half an hour later, during another contraction, the iron knocker tapped on the front door and Mary led Mrs Collins the midwife into the room.

'Thought it might be good to arrive early,' Mrs Collins said.

'And I need to keep an eye on the boys,' Mary said. 'I don't want anything strange happening in here if you're alone.'

Eva leaned onto the rail of a high-back chair and did not answer.

'Looks like I've arrived just in time,' Mrs Collins said. She handed her large carpet bag to Mary and held Eva's hand until she could walk her to the stairs.

'Keep the kettle filled and boiling,' she said to Mary over her shoulder.

Eva stepped onto the bottom stair, with Mrs Collins' arm about her waist, and grinned when she heard Mary mutter, 'You'd think I had no idea what to do.'

After Eva laboured for a total of seven hours, and heaved for twenty minutes, Mrs Evans tied off and cut the umbilical cord of a wide-eyed, peaceful baby. She wrapped the child in white linen, and lay Eva's third son into her arms.

Perhaps because of the letter that day. Perhaps she would have anyway, Eva decided that this boy would take one of the names of the young man who'd saved her. None of her children would have been born without the bravery of that midshipman just over ten years ago and she was fairly sure this child would be her last.

Eva named her third son Richard and left her husband to choose the child's two middle names.

She'd tell Tom in her reply.

Eva looked into her tiny son's eyes and knew that she and Tom had each truly found their own places in the world.

The *Loch Ard*
1873–1878

CAST OF CHARACTERS

Ages are shown if known and are based on approximate age in

May 1878.

(Round brackets for 'also known as', or another option of name.)

[Square brackets for author's edit of name.]

See frontispiece for disclaimer.

FACTUAL CHARACTERS

CREW

1. George Gibb: Captain, 29, from Kincardine, UK
2. Thomas [Mac] McLauchlan: first-mate, 43, from London, UK
3. George Baxter: second-mate, 27, from Glasgow, UK
4. Ernest Atkinson: third-mate, 21
5. James Rancie: carpenter, 36, from Aberdeen, UK
6. Richard Hunt: boatswain, 41, from London, UK
7. Robert Fox: sailmaker, 31, from Glasgow, UK
8. George Clay: steward, purser, 53, from Devonport, UK
9. Rowland Giles: cook, 33, from Cheltenham, UK
10. Thomas Heselton: able seaman, 42, from Hull, UK
11. G. McNeil: able seaman, 22, from Glasgow, UK
12. John McGennily (or McGemily): able seaman, 25

13. E. Vedel: able seaman, 21, from Denmark, Europe
14. A.M. Grangoest: (or N.M. Grangvist): able seaman, 22, from Sweden, Europe
15. John Johnston, (or Johnson): able seaman, 23, from Denmark, Europe
16. John Egan: able seaman, 37
17. Charles Cameron: able seaman, 30
18. George Freeman: able seaman, 29, from Devonport, UK
19. Joseph King: able seaman, 23, from London, UK
20. William Legg: able seaman, 35
21. William Wright: able seaman, 23
22. George Skinner: able seaman, 23
23. John Brooks: able seaman, 24
24. Thomas King: able seaman, 25
25. George Smith: able seaman, 23, from Wick, UK
26. James Wood, able seaman, 34
27. Henry Anderson: able seaman
28. C. Archer: able seaman, 30
29. Magnus Murray: able seaman, 21, from Shetland, UK
30. E.F. Finchman (or F.T. Fincham): ordinary seaman, 17
31. Henry Donohue: engine-driver, 27
32. William [Billy] Johnson: lamptrimmer, cook's mate, 29
33. Charles Spicer: second steward, 19
34. Robert [Straz] Strasenburgh: apprentice, 18, from Leith, UK
35. William Stevenson: apprentice, 17
36. Robert Smith: able seaman, 45

37. Thomas (Tom) Pearce (previously Millett): apprentice, 18, from Melbourne, Australia

PASSENGERS

1. Evory Carmichael snr: doctor, 45 (?), from Cork
2. Rebecca Carmichael: wife of Evory snr, 45
3. Rebecca (Raby) Carmichael: eldest daughter, 21
4. Eveline (Eva) Carmichael: daughter, 19
5. Evory Carmichael jnr: son, 16
6. Thomas Carmichael: son, 14
7. Margaret Carmichael: daughter, 10
8. Anne [Annie] Carmichael: daughter, 6
9. John Stuckey: 25, from Oxford
10. Francis (or Frances) Stuckey: wife of John, 23
11. Reginald Jones: 26, from Kent
12. George Yates: 36
13. Thomas Pitt: 37
14. William Patterson
15. Herbert Godley
16. Gerard Rolleston: 17
17. Arthur [Art] Mitchell: 25, from Scotland

OTHER FACTUAL CHARACTERS

- William Carmichael: son of Dr Carmichael, 24, from Ireland
- James Collingwood: unknown. He is listed on the passenger list at *Loch Ard* cemetery, but not on any other passenger or crew list.

- Hugh Gibson: farmer of Glenample, 51, from Ayr, UK
- Lavinia Gibson: wife of Hugh
- George Ford: shepherd/employee of Hugh Gibson
- W. [Wally] Till: shepherd/employee of Hugh Gibson
- Constable Graham: police officer at Camperdown
- Constable Swale: police officer at Camperdown
- Mr McIntyre: missionary at Heytesbury Forest
- Mr Blythe: shipping agent
- Emily Mayne: Tom Pearce's mother, and Tom's three sisters and a brother
- E.G. Williams [Edgar]: Tom's uncle by marriage
- Mrs Williams [Doreen]: Tom's mother's sister, his aunt
- Sir George Bowen, Governor of Victoria
- Thomas Achilles [Archie] Townshend: husband of Eva Carmichael, and their children Philip, Francis and Richard
- Edith Gurney Strasenburgh: sister of Robert Strasenburgh, wife of Tom Pearce, and their children Thomas, Robert and Edith May

SOME FICTITIOUS CHARACTERS

- Alice and Eliza, housekeepers at Glenample
- Jack, boy worker at Glenample
- Station master at Geelong
- Harry Edwards: journalist, Melbourne

- The Three Daws Inn
  - In existence since the 15th Century.
  - In 2023, still open at Town Pier, Gravesend, Kent.
- The Clipper Ship – *Loch Ard*
  - An iron ship built in Yard 87 at Glasgow by Connell & Co. Official number 68061.
  - Launched 8 November 1873. Flag: GBR (Great Britain).
  - 1,623 tonnage.
  - Three-masted clipper.
  - Length 262.7 feet; width 38.3 feet; depth draft 23 feet.
  - Owned by General Shipping Co. (Aitken & Lilburn, Managers) Glasgow.
  - On this voyage, carried 3,275 tons of cargo valued at £54,000 and insured for £30,000. Cargo included items such as perfumes, pianos, clocks, linen, candles, confectionery, umbrellas and straw hats plus industrial items such as railway irons, lead, cement and copper.
- The Flagstaff Hill Maritime Museum in Warrnambool keeps a collection of artefacts (in 2023), including the Minton Peacock.
- The Port Campbell Visitor Information Centre also features relics and an interesting display about the ship and its history.

Note from the Author

Below is a selection of the resources used to develop this novel. They are in alphabetical order.

(Because weblinks have lives of their own, they are not listed as web addresses here.)

- Ancestry dot com dot au
- Bureau of Meteorology (Australia) Climate and Ocean Data Services
- *Clipper Ship* by John O'Hara Cosgrave II
- *Clipper Ships and the Golden Age of Sail* by Sam Jefferson
- *Dictionary of Disasters at Sea* by Charles Hocking F.L.A.
- Environment dot gov dot au: wreck dive information
- Find My Past dot com dot au
- Google images
- Google maps
- Museums Victoria
- National Library of Australia *Trove*, for example:
  - The *Age* newspaper (Melbourne)
  - The *Argus* newspaper (Melbourne)
  - The *Ballarat Courier* newspaper (VIC)
  - The *Ballarat Star* newspaper (VIC)
  - The *Geelong Advertiser* newspaper (VIC)
  - The *Herald* newspaper (Melbourne)
  - The *Sydney Morning Herald* newspaper (NSW)
- Newspapers dot com
- *The Times* newspaper (London)
- *Out at Sea: The Emigrant Afloat* by P.B. Chadfield

- Public Record Office London
- State Library of Victoria
- Thames Tugs dot co dot UK
- *The Otways* by Trevor Pescott
- Three Daws dot co dot UK
- *To Auckland by the Ganges* by Robert M. Grogans
- Victorian Collections dot net dot au has an excellent diagram of the *Loch Ard*
- Wikipedia, (please be aware that Wikipedia is 'crowd sourced' and not all information within it is factually accurate and is often edited). Some pages used as base research were:
  - *Thomas Richard Pearce* (Wikipedia page says he was born in Ireland but other ancestry research – including his promotion certificates – name Melbourne)
  - *Loch Ard Gorge*
  - *Loch Ard (ship)*
  - *SS Gothenburg*

ABOUT THE AUTHOR

Jackie Randall is a storyteller who researches historical events to bring people and their stories back from the past.

Born in England, Jackie now lives with her husband Phillip on a small rural property north of Sydney, Australia. They have three amazing adult children who now each have their own beautiful families.

Jackie Randall is also the author of *Emelin* − medieval historical fiction for readers aged 9-plus − and is a contributor to the *Dust Makers* anthology that investigates sustainability through a variety of short stories.